COPYCAT KILLER

A SHELF INDULGENCE COZY MYSTERY

S.E. BABIN

OLIVERHEBERBOOKS

Previously published by Sweet Promise Press - 2019

Published by Oliver-Heber Books

0 9 8 7 6 5 4 3 2 1

ONE

Poppy the Persian was getting on my last nerve. For some reason, she hadn't liked a single person who'd come into the shop today and decided to make her displeasure known. Loudly.

After about the fifth yowl, I glared at the cat. She returned my stare with a haughty look of her own and Poppy's tail went up straight into the air as she turned and showed me her butt. Harper, my assistant, tried to cough to cover her laugh, but she wasn't too successful at it. I frowned at her as I shooed Poppy away.

The grumpy cat was usually a popular staple in Tattered Pages, my funky little bookshop smack in the middle of Silverwood Hollow, but lately, she'd been a loud wreck of a pet. I'd taken her to the vet, much to her extreme dismay, had them run a barrage of tests which resulted in me eating beans and rice for a few weeks because it cost so much, only to find out Poppy wasn't even a little sick.

She was just a temperamental jerk.

I thought about downgrading to the cheap cat food just to teach her a lesson, but I wasn't that cruel. After the fourth night of leftovers, though, I wondered just how much I could save from downgrading from Fancy Feast to Budget Bites.

Today was worse than usual and the timing of Poppy's outburst coincided with the most stressful day I'd had in a while. My shop was hosting Mary Ruth Steinman, a cozy mystery author who'd shot to fame with her story of a young sleuth and a knitting chihuahua. In my opinion, which no one cared about, if you slapped a puppy or a cat on a cover, nine times out of ten it would be a hit. There was just something about an adorable pet that hit the heart and the purse strings just right. The real thing could be just as good, but right now, with my grumpy Persian yowling at the top of her lungs, I was disinclined to be excited about the upcoming guest. Or anything else, for that matter.

The author would be here in a few hours, so Harper and I were doing our best to make sure the shop was in tip-top shape. We hosted a lot of authors in the shop, but most of them were from surrounding towns or the state of Virginia. It was rare we hosted an out of towner with as much clout as Mary Ruth, and I found it odd she'd chosen our little shop out of all the other larger, more well-known bookshops in the state. Not that I was complaining. Once

I'd announced the signing, business at Tattered Pages had gone up 25%, especially with tourists, and we were booked solid for the event.

Harper wore her trademark messy bun today and an old Aerosmith t-shirt with a pair of skinny jeans with holes in the knees. I'd given her the ol' raised eyebrow when she walked in, but Harper merely rolled her eyes and held up the bag she carried in her other hand.

"Change of clothes in here," she said before I could speak. "Really, Dakota. After all these years, you still don't trust me?"

Guilt filled me at her words. I took a breath to apologize, but Harper snorted and waved her hand at me. "I enjoy your paranoia most of the time," she said as she hung up the garment bag, "but I'll let you off the hook today. This would stress me out, too."

And it did. The local news would be here in an hour and if Poppy didn't shut her yapper, this event would go down in history as Silverwood Hollow's worst local celebrity event in history. Or maybe the *only* celebrity event. This was the first time I could remember the town hosting someone of her caliber. And she wasn't huge or anything - no Stephen King or anything like that, but her star was rising fast.

Along with the rumors.

I rarely booked an author I didn't thoroughly research and, considering I was a book and somewhat of a tech nerd, I knew how to deep dive into online research. Mary Ruth was quite the controversial figure if you dug deep enough.

Accusations of plagiarism plagued her more than once, though the charges never came to fruition. People accused her publishers of throwing money at the problem and burying the accusers in legal bills. Unfortunately, this was true more often than not, so I'd tucked away those tidbits and thought I'd see for myself. I hadn't spoken to Mary Ruth yet, just her agent - a young, fidgety woman who seemed constantly on edge. She spoke faster than I could comprehend, and after asking her three times to repeat herself, the woman finally slowed down enough to tell me what she wanted.

I could put up with a lot if it meant more business for the shop, so I'd agreed to host the signing and within days a huge shipment of mass-market paperbacks landed on my doorstep with instructions threatening me not to let a single book out of my sight. What I hadn't known then was this was Mary Ruth's release party. If I'd known that, I might not have been so inclined to jump at the opportunity. Now the pressure was tenfold. They sprang that one on me, but I went along with it, grateful for the boost in business.

The phone in the shop rang, startling me out of my thoughts. Daydreaming wouldn't get me anywhere, and I had way too much to do to start lollygagging. I snatched up the phone. "Tattered Pages," I chirped into the receiver.

"Word on the street is you got a nosy nelly telling everyone about plagiarism accusations against Mary Ruth Steinman. Care to give the first word to your friendly neighborhood journalist?" The voice on the line was deeply amused and belonged to one of my good friends, Cole Gardner.

"Cole, I don't have time for this today. She's going to be here in just a little while."

Cole gasped like he was deeply offended. "Dakota Adair snubs small town journalist. Expose at five o'clock," he said dramatically.

My lips twitched and trying to keep my voice stern was useless. A laugh bubbled out of me. "What do you want?"

"Touchy, touchy. I'm just calling to see how you're doing. You really do have a nosy nelly telling everyone who'll listen about Mary Ruth. What's that about?" His tone sounded intrigued, which made me put my guard up. Cole was a good friend, but still a journalist, so I had to be careful with what I shared. This put boundaries on our friendship, which wasn't great, but as long as Cole worked for the Silverwood Hollow Gazette, I had to watch what I said around him. We'd gotten past some of that after I'd cleared him of murder a few months ago, but he still worked as a journalist and as long as he did, I'd watch what I said lest I wind up in the paper.

"You know how rumors get started," I said airily. "Thanks for checking on me, but I really do have to go."

"Lunch tomorrow," Cole interjected, before I could hang up. "Same time. Same place. I'll bring cider. You bring chicken salad."

"Done. I really have to go."

"Fare thee well, Miss Adair," Cole said with a wistful sigh. "Parting is such sweet -"

I hung up the phone even as I couldn't hide the smile curling my lips. When I first met Cole, he was stalking a crime scene and me by association because I was there. I'd thought he was cute, but knew to be wary of men seeking information. Especially handsome ones. But as we worked together on the case, we'd become good friends. Now we had a standing lunch date once a month where we'd set a rule that neither of us could talk about business. No books. No news.

Just Cole and Dakota, chatting about our lives.

It was nice having a friend like that.

Of course, the lines between friendship and something else had gotten a tiny bit blurred while I helped solve a murder for him, but our relationship had cooled once I realized he was seeing a woman who wasn't all that nice. It didn't help she'd wound up dead. He wasn't guilty. I knew that. It was hard to get over, though, especially since he hadn't told me about her, and I found it all out through sleuthing. It wasn't my business, but we were friends, right? You'd think he would have mentioned dating someone if they'd been together for a while. So... we were still friends. We still had lunch. But there was a boundary there that hadn't been there before.

The bell over the door jangled and in rushed a tiny, harried woman. The door banged her on the hip, and she winced but kept plowing through until she'd plopped the pile of boxes she was holding on top of the checkout counter.

"Hi, Betty," I said politely as I scooted the boxes out

of my field of vision. Betty Jones was about five feet nothing but had a mouth as big as a skyscraper. The woman chattered incessantly. It didn't matter what the subject was, Betty Jones could chat you to the moon and back about it.

"Hey Dakota," she said, out of breath as she leaned against the counter. "This is the last of the debut books. Mary Ruth signed all of them, so you can charge a few bucks more for them."

One of the perks of having Mary Ruth in the shop today was the percentage of sales I'd get from her books. My cozy mystery section in the store was on the small side, but we made a point to keep it well stocked with local authors. Since Mary Ruth's debut hadn't released yet, I knew it would be a hot seller.

"Great!" I said just as Betty opened her mouth again. I needed to distract her so I could get some work done. I took one of the boxes and made my way to the display table at the front of the store. "I'll set these up here. If you want to go ahead and check out Mary Ruth's table, it's over there." As soon as I set the boxes down, I pointed to the back of the store.

Betty frowned at me. I couldn't get trapped in a conversation with her. The last time I did, I got stuck there for so long, I thought my bones would crumble into dust.

"She'll be here in about an hour, so if you want to get a good seat, I'd grab one now!"

Betty stared at me with suspicion, but hurried off when I smiled encouragingly at her. She always liked being first at everything. I couldn't help if I abused that knowledge a little.

I slumped against the counter when she was out of sight. Harper snorted and nudged me with her elbow. "It will be okay. Mary Ruth is bringing in a lot of business today, but she'll be out of our hair by dinner time."

I gave her a weak smile. "Let's hope." Part of me felt a little funny having her sign here knowing her history. I'd fielded a few calls with angry townspeople over it, but people wanted her book, and I needed the business. In the future, maybe I'd have more power to resist these kinds of calls. Now, though, I still had a lot of growing to do before I could. Plus, I had to compete with Binders, a cool bookshop over in Candlelight Springs. Harriet, the owner, was proving to have some serious marketing chops.

She'd taken me under her wing since I'd help put the killer away. Harriet's bookstore parking lot was the scene of the crime and Harriet had been beside herself trying to get her business back up. I'd helped figure out who the killer was, and Binders was now back up and running.

Harriet urged me to take Mary Ruth on. I jumped at the opportunity, but now looking around the shop, I felt stressed and tired and everything but happy about this. Harper squeezed my shoulder and turned me.

"Look," she whispered.

Trudy, my friend and owner of Sprinkle Heaven, pushed the door to Tattered Pages open with her hip and came in bearing a massive tray of muffins. Behind her, a young woman carried a huge industrial coffee server and the person behind her had a large box.

Tears filled my eyes.

Trudy saw me and smiled widely until she saw my expression. She rushed in, setting the box down on the register. "Oh honey, don't cry. My muffins aren't that bad."

A wet snort escaped me. "Trudy, this is wonderful. Really, really wonderful."

"Thank Harper," Trudy said. "You didn't even tell me you had a signing!"

I'd been too busy to do anything other than plan this thing. I smiled apologetically. "I'm so sorry. This is my first event and I've been overwhelmed. Planning things might not be for me."

Trudy patted me on the hand. "Honey, that's why you have to delegate." Her gaze flicked over to Harper. "We have to use the talents of people put in our path."

I'd just given Harper a raise, but maybe I'd have to reexamine this after the signing. "Harper is amazing," I admitted.

Harper preened a little and snickered before she left us to chat. I stared after her. "She has a lot more potential than a small bookstore in a small town."

Trudy sighed. "Honey, sometimes that's all people want." She gave me a meaningful look. "Just make sure you don't take her for granted."

"I just gave her a raise." I snickered and lowered my voice. "Probably wasn't enough after the Mary Ruth storm."

"That bad?" Trudy motioned for her companions to carry their loads over to the back. "Just set them down on the tables Harper set up."

"I haven't even met the woman yet. Can you believe that?" I rubbed my hands over my eyes and groaned. "She'll be here in a little while."

"Only a few hours. Then you'll be free of her." Trudy hoisted the muffin containers. I took one of them. "Let me, please. It's the least I can do."

"I'm ready for a bath and bedtime," I said as we walked over. "As soon as this is done, I'm closing up shop and soaking in a tub full of bubbles."

"Sounds like heaven." Trudy opened the container and the scent of blueberries and caramelized sugar wafted up.

"Your muffins are truly miraculous," I said to her. I reached down to grab one, but she smacked me lightly on the hand.

"Nope. Those are for customers." She took me by the hand. "I have something else for you."

Trudy led me back to the front and rummaged through her massive purse. She pulled out a brown paper bag and handed it over. "You need something more than a muffin."

I opened it and peered inside. Cookies. Loads and loads of cookies. Chocolate ones. My mouth watered as the heavenly scent drifted up to me.

"Bless you," I said with feeling. Just then, the door opened and a tall, large boned woman walked in holding a chihuahua. She had an air about her, a look that told me she'd do whatever she could to make you do what she wanted. You needed a friend? That's what she'd be. A confidante? You betcha. But I also got the vibe the second you stopped doing what she wanted or questioned something, you became persona non grata.

Mary Ruth Steinman had arrived. Her red hair was piled on top of her hair with a glittery clip. She wore a pair of blue slacks and a flowy white shirt. Her glasses perched on top of her head, and she wore little makeup. Lip gloss and some mascara. Her nose was hawkish and above them her dark eyes flitted to and fro.

She saw Harper before me. "Excuse me?" Her voice was higher than I expected it to be.

I chewed on my lip as I thought about what to do with the chihuahua. Considering I had a cat in here, I didn't know if I had a lot of ground to stand on, but it was my store, so there was that.

Harper looked up. Her expression went blank for a second before she plastered the fakest smile I'd ever seen on her face. "Miss Steinman?" She got up from her seat and walked over to her. Harper took the box Mary Ruth held. "We have a room all set up for you in the back so you can take a few moments."

"Do you have coffee?" she asked.

Thank all the heavens above for Trudy being an angel. And thank Harper for being better at this than me. Harper's gaze slid my way, and I caught the amused twinkle in them. "We sure do. Would you like to follow me?"

Mary Ruth didn't even look at me as she breezed past. I watched them go, took a deep breath, and decided to wait a minute before I went back there to talk to her. This had all been such a pain that I was ready to get it over with, but there wasn't much I'd rather not do than socialize with people I didn't know.

I gave Harper a minute before I walked to the back. Betty caught my eye. She sat in the front row, a self-satisfied smirk on her face. I nodded to her and headed to the room Harper set up for Mary Ruth.

I knocked a couple of times and poked my head in. Harper stood with her back to the wall, an expression on her face I'd never seen before. The chihuahua growled at my assistant.

"Hello," I said as I stepped in. What in the world was happening here? "I'm Dakota Adair, owner of Tattered Pages. You must be Mary Ruth." I slapped a friendly smile on my face.

"You should have been here to greet me," Mary Ruth sniffed. "Not your assistant." She said the word like she'd stepped on something unsavory.

I blinked at her. Was this lady for real? "Harper is a valued employee. Not to mention my only one. She's the face for every event I have." The lie came out straight faced. This was the only real event I'd held here since I opened the place, but she didn't need to know that.

"Well, I expect you to come and greet me next time my publicist sets something like this up."

There won't be a next time, the little devil inside of me said snidely.

"I'm here now," I said with extreme patience. "I hope

you're getting settled in. We have coffee and muffins outside. If you'd like some, I'd be happy to get it for you."

Mary Ruth sat on the couch we'd brought in just for this signing. "I'd like a latte, please. Caramel, two pumps of vanilla syrup, one pump of hazelnut. Whipped cream on top."

This was Binders deja vu. "I'm sorry," I said, though I knew I didn't sound sorry at all. "The only thing we have out there is a great French roast and decaf. But Trudy's muffins make up for that. She's the best baker and coffee maker we have around here."

Mary Ruth glared. "My instructions were sent over to you two days before I booked this signing."

I had no idea what she was talking about. "I can assure you, I didn't receive any special instructions from anyone." I smiled with regret. "Though if I had, I might have had to ask you to sign somewhere else. We don't have a lot of flexibility to accommodate special requests. It is a small town, after all." I'd rather eat Brussel sprouts for a week than accommodate any of this terrible woman's requests. Maybe if she was nicer...

Her face went beet red as she processed my words. "Do you know who I am?"

I made my expression as blank as I could. Harper still pressed herself against the wall. "Well, I hope your name is Mary Ruth Steinman, because if it isn't, we have an issue, don't we!" I smiled at her. "Would you like me to go double check the books we have to make sure you're at the right place?"

Outside the door, I heard the sound of choked laughter.

"I've never been treated so -!"

Her voice cut off right away as Detective Hardy Cavanaugh stepped into the room. I kept my smile steady as I watched emotions play over Mary Ruth's face. Hardy took a lot of people's breath away, myself included, so I didn't begrudge the woman a little shock, but when I noticed avarice flash in her eyes, I stood up a little straighter.

"Hello, Detective Cavanaugh," I said.

His eyebrow went up a little at the greeting. We'd moved from titles to first names a while ago. He only used Miss when he got mad at me, and I used Detective when I wanted to annoy him. Except for today.

"Miss Adair," he said, playing along. "Harper." He nodded to her before his gaze drifted back to Mary Ruth, who'd stood up and was smoothing her hair.

She smiled then, a completely different look than the smile she wore earlier. "Hello," she breathed and held out her hand. "I'm Mary Ruth Steinman. Dakota was so gracefully offering to get me a cup of coffee. Would you like one?"

My brows rose. Hardy blinked. "I'm fully equipped to get my own, thank you, but I'd be happy to grab it for you. Dakota here looks like she's swamped."

At the mention of my name, her lips turned down and her eyes turned angry. The chihuahua yipped in her arms.

Hardy glanced down at the dog. "Well now, what do we have here?"

The chihuahua wagged its tail. "I'd pet you," he said to the dog, "but I'm more of a cat man myself."

He stepped out to get her coffee, leaving me alone with the fuming author. "Who is that?"

"He just told you," Harper said, her voice dripping with annoyance. She checked her watch. "We have ten minutes before we need to start. Is there anything else you need?" From the tone of her voice, you could tell she'd rather give herself a thousand paper cuts and take a salt-water bath than do anything to help Mary Ruth. I stifled a smile.

Hardy came back in holding two cups of coffee. "Trudy makes the best coffee around." He held one out to her. "I'm sure you'll agree."

She took it, careful to brush her fingers against his. "I'm sure I will."

"Well," I said. "I'll leave you to get settled, then. I'll pop back in when it's a couple minutes to start."

Mary Ruth nodded, distracted. We turned to leave, but she cleared her throat. "If Detective Cavanaugh can stay? I'm working on a new novel and could use the advice of someone in law enforcement. It's rare I have someone... at my disposal."

My smile turned brittle. I looked over at Hardy, who looked like he'd swallowed a lemon. Clearing my throat, I spoke. "Of course. I'm sure he wouldn't mind helping."

Harper and I left them and hurried out of the room.

Most of the seats had already filled. More people were milling around, browsing through the shelves. When we got back up to the register, Harper let out an exasperated sigh.

"She is the worst!" she hissed.

"That she is." I checked my cell phone. "We have an hour for the talk and an hour and a half for the signing. We can do this."

Harper groaned. "Speak for yourself."

TWO

Things started out well. Mary Ruth came out, Hardy at her heels. I pretended not to notice the possessive hand she laid on him right before she settled in at the table like a queen bee. An air of quiet anticipation settled over the room. I had to hand it to her. She knew how to wait and how to milk the crowd. The noise level grew, and she waited to speak until it died down to quiet whispers.

Harper busied herself with making sure all the copies of her newest book were stacked neatly on a table right in front of the register. The Knitting Chihuahua series felt a little odd to me, but she had a loyal fanbase. From the amount of people crammed into the shop, that fanbase was larger than I thought it was.

Once Mary Ruth began to speak, I turned my attention to other things.

Hardy hung around for a while and when he was ready to leave, he motioned me over. I put down the books

S.E. BABIN

I was stocking and headed over to the door. My heartbeat picked up a little faster as I approached.

We'd gone out to see an Agatha Christie play a few nights ago. It wasn't a date, but it was kind of a date. It felt like Hardy mostly wanted to get the peace back between us after Cole had been picked up for murder. It did the trick, but a tension that hadn't been there before lurked between us now.

Plus, I couldn't deny how handsome and available he was, even as I knew getting involved wasn't what I wanted. Not right now anyway.

He leaned forward, his breath tickling my ear. "She's a real piece of work, isn't she?"

I sighed and looked over at the author. Her hands waved animatedly around as she read from her book. The crowd laughed. "She's good at this."

He nodded. "Manipulators usually are."

I glanced up at him sharply. "Those are strong words."

Hardy stared at Mary Ruth for a long moment, his jaw clenched. "I see people like her every day in my line of work. She surrounds herself with people who give her what she wants. The second someone questions her, she turns it around and plays the victim."

I felt much the same way about her. "She's only here for today. Once this is over, I plan to be much more discerning about the people I bring in to sign."

"Probably not a bad idea." His gaze trailed over the people sitting around Mary Ruth. "Though you have a full house today with this one."

18

I opened my mouth to speak.

"Mary Ruth, my name is Martha Hemming." I glanced over at her. She was a regular at Tattered Pages. I'd never had any trouble with her, and I always thought she was a kind sort. Her dark hair was done up today in a neat high bun and her bangs brushed away from her face. Her eyes were pinched at the edges and her face held an anger I'd never seen before. She clenched and unclenched the fists resting at her sides. "I wrote a book last year about a knitting chihuahua and sent it over to an alpha reader for some feedback."

Mary Ruth's face went bone white for a second. She composed herself quickly and sat up a little straighter. "Did you now?" Her smile was cool and polite.

Martha nodded. "As you well know, I did. I find it interesting that several months later, I heard about a new and well-reviewed cozy mystery about a knitting chihuahua."

Mary Ruth's smile dropped. The crowd shifted in their seats to turn and look at Martha. "I'm sure you've thought about the consequences of accusing me of something as serious as plagiarism, haven't you?"

Martha stood her ground. "It's also interesting to me to find out the alpha reader I sent my work to was none other than Betty Jones."

Betty's head dropped for a moment.

Martha gave a triumphant smile. "I think you know Betty Jones very well, don't you? After all, she is your assistant, isn't she?"

A collective gasp sounded in the room, me included. The evidence against Mary Ruth felt damning. Mary's eyes blinked rapidly for a moment before she stood up.

"I've never seen a copy of your manuscript or had anything to do with Betty's alpha reading side project." Mary Ruth shrugged. "I'm way too busy to read other people's work and make it a practice not to do that any way. It's too easy for the lines to cross."

Martha snorted. "Really now? That's what you're claiming?" Her gaze shifted to Betty. "Do you have anything to say about this?"

Betty's gaze shifted away from Martha. "No. I always make sure I keep my advanced reading copies away from other people. It never left my possession."

"Uh huh," Martha said. "You don't think it's a little strange that my entire plot wound up in Mary Ruth's new book?"

Hardy stepped forward, but I put a hand on his arm. "I'll handle it," I whispered. Just as I began walking toward Mary Ruth, she stood up.

"Accusing me of stealing at my own book signing?" she hissed. "That's low even for a backwoods northerner."

The mood of the room shifted from shock to anger. Silverwood Hollow didn't take kindly to outsiders insulting their own.

"Excuse me?" Martha screeched. "The only back-woods northerner here is you and you're a thief to boot!"

Martha and Mary Ruth started forward just as I slid in

between them. "Excuse me, ladies and gentlemen, I'm so sorry about this, but I think it's time to shut this down."

"I'll sue you!" Martha screamed.

"Try it! You have no case to stand on!" Mary Ruth screamed back. "I'll bury you in legal bills and red tape!"

"Ha!" Martha screamed back. "So you admit it then!"

"I don't have a need for your books. Mine stand on their own!" Mary Ruth surged forward. I stumbled and put my hands out, only for an iron grip to lock around my arm.

"That's enough," Hardy's voice rumbled over me.

"She's accusing me of theft!" Mary Ruth screeched.

"It's not an accusation if it's true!" Martha screeched back. "It's a fact!"

"Everyone out," Hardy barked, his hand still locked over my arm.

"What about our books?" someone shouted from the back.

Hardy glared at Mary Ruth hard. "I'm sure the author will be gracious to sign all of your copies before she leaves. If you want a signed copy, grab a sticky note from Harper and put your name and phone number in it. Before she leaves, we'll have her sign one and call you when it's ready."

Most everyone grumbled, but they all got out of their seats and headed toward the door. Harper snapped into action and handed out sticky notes and pens to the people who wanted their books signed. I noticed not many people handed them over. I also noticed several people putting their copies back on the stand. I bit down my frustrated sigh.

Betty, Martha, and Mary Ruth remained behind. Betty detoured around the back of us to stand behind Mary Ruth.

"Martha," Hardy said, "if you want to continue this, you need to take it out of Dakota's shop."

Martha's face turned beet red. "She stole my life's work!"

"A knitting chihuahua is your life's work?" Mary Ruth sneered. "That's sad. It's a dog. With no opposable thumbs!"

Martha's mouth fell open. She closed it and her expression went apoplectic. "You just used it to make a buck!" Martha squeezed her eyes shut. "You think it's stupid, but you wrote it anyway knowing it could be marketable."

"I don't have to steal any of your work," Mary Ruth snapped. "Anyone could have thought of that!"

Martha pulled out a copy of the Mary Ruth's book. Multi-colored tabs littered the edges of it. "But could they have thought of the Twisted Needle shop?" She flipped through the book. "Or the Java De-Lite shop?" Tears formed in her eyes. "Those are the exact places in my manuscript. Don't you have any shame?"

Mary Ruth shoved past me and Hardy. "I don't need shame," she hissed. "All I have to do is look at my bank account each day and know I've won."

The book dropped from Martha's hand. I stared at

Mary Ruth in shock. Hardy's hand loosened its grip. By now, all the people had left the shop. Harper stood a few feet away, her eyes wide.

A tear fell down Martha's face.

I brushed past them all and over to the door. I held it open. "I want you to leave. Now."

Martha glared back at Mary Ruth but walked out the door after a moment, her head held high.

"I'm not leaving until I get my property back," Mary Ruth snapped.

I counted to five in my head so I wouldn't say something terrible. Harper stepped in so I didn't have to.

"I'm so sorry, Mrs. Steinman. We have none of your property. The books sent to us came direct from your publisher."

A wide, genuine smile crossed Harper's face then. "But we do have people who've paid for your book." She frowned down at the small pile on the table next to the door. "Although it wasn't quite what we thought it would be, your fans are still requesting your signature on these." She handed one over with a pen. "If you'd like to take care of that before you leave, that would be great."

Mary Ruth bared her teeth at Harper and was about to say something more than likely blistering, so I stepped in and cleared my throat. "We have an agreement with your publisher about these books and this signing. It's in your contract to ensure a signing is done."

"You didn't have the signing!" Mary Ruth snapped.

"It's also in my contract that if anything happens in my shop I feel might endanger my customers, I'm well within my rights to shut it down." I held her gaze until she looked away.

Mary Ruth sent a questioning look to Betty. Her assistant shrugged. "She's the only bookstore in this town and since your book was set here, it wouldn't surprise me..." her voice trailed off.

"I'll be speaking with my publisher asap," Mary Ruth growled, snatching the book out of Harper's hands. Harper responded by picking up another stack and setting them in front of her.

We stood in awkward silence for a few minutes as she signed all of them. Hardy stood at my back, a welcome and comforting source of safety. As soon as she finished, Harper smiled politely. "Thanks so much. I hope you have a wonderful day."

"Oh sod off," Mary Ruth snapped as she tugged her purse over her shoulder and sailed out the door, Betty following meekly behind her.

When the door shut, Harper rushed over to lock it and sagged against it.

"I can't believe how smart you were to get a contract with that publisher."

I grinned at her and pulled a chair over before sagging into it. I kicked off my sandals. "I didn't."

Harper's eyes widened. Hardy burst into surprised laughter.

A tired chuckle slipped from me. "I'm sure I'll hear about that one later."

"But not today," Harper said, her mouth twitching in amusement.

"Not today," I agreed with a sigh.

THREE

The next morning, Cole stood at the front door to the shop before I'd even opened. I slid out of my Rav4 and shook my head.

"No comment," I said as a greeting.

Cole smiled so wide his bright green eyes crinkled at the edges. "Now come on. Is that any way to treat a friend?"

"It's the way I treat a journalist masquerading as a friend this early."

His smile slipped just a hair. To his credit, he slipped his notebook and pen back into his pocket. "Harsh, Dakota."

"I haven't had my first cup of coffee yet and I find you standing here with your notepad in your hand and a camera around your neck. Now tell me, who's the harsh one here?"

Cole waited until I unlocked the door and stepped in behind me. "I'm just trying to do my job."

"And I'm trying to do mine," I said as I tugged my jacket, scarf, and hat off and hung them on the rack. "I don't want reporters milling around here. If you're here as Cole, you're always welcome. If you're trying to get a scoop out of me, I'm afraid you're going to find this source all dried up."

Cole held his hands up. "Fine. I surrender." He slid his jacket and scarf off as well, but kept them tucked over his arm. "Tell me what happened."

One of my eyebrows rose. Cole rolled his eyes. "Off the record. Cole to Dakota. Scout's honor."

"Were you a scout?"

Cole chuckled. "I was, and I take that oath seriously. Now, tell me as a friend. Are you okay?"

I waved a hand. "I'm fine. It was a disagreement. That's all. Harper and I handled it in a few minutes."

Cole gave me a look. "Only a disagreement? I heard it was a lot more intense than that. Martha accused the woman of plagiarizing her novel?"

I nodded. "She did. Sounds like she might have a case, too."

He made a curious noise. "Hmm. I think so. I ran into Martha last night. She told me not only did she send the book to Betty, she also shopped it to Mary Ruth's agent to see if she could get a deal."

I ran my hand over my face. "Are you kidding? How in the world did Mary Ruth think she'd get away with that?"

Cole chuckled. "Sometimes people forget they're merely human. Maybe her ego got too big, and she thought she was untouchable."

"This is a disaster," I groaned. "I just hope my business doesn't suffer for it."

I still had around fifteen minutes before opening. I'd been checking Google and Yelp reviews after the Mary Ruth disaster, but so far people were being kind. Not a single person left a bad review. I didn't think I would have escaped if I'd charged money for the signing, but I made it free with the requirement they purchase the book from here if they wanted it signed. Speaking of which... I frowned over at the pile of unsold books sitting on the table. If I didn't move some copies of it today, I might have to package them all and send them back to the publisher.

A picture of money on fire appeared in my head and I tried to suppress it. There wasn't anything I could do about it now, so I didn't see any reason to fret about it. Even though it would have been nice to have a little boost in my bank account... A sigh escaped me.

"Don't worry. You'll be fine. Everyone loves you around here." Cole flipped through the newest stack of thrillers. "I think you might be persona non grata with her publisher though."

"Thanks for that," I said. I sent a glare at his back. "It's not my fault they contracted a cheater."

"It could take years for this all to resolve. Most of it will probably fall onto Mary Ruth's shoulders. The publisher protects itself from charges like these with the way they write their contracts." He snorted. "Usually," he added. "You know I have to write something about this in the paper, right?"

"Yes." I didn't quite snap the word, but it was a close thing. "Just make sure you add in we're having a thirty percent sale this week," I added as an afterthought.

Cole laughed. "I'll do my best."

Business didn't suffer that day. People milled in right when the doors opened and kept up a steady trickle until around three that afternoon. Closing time fell at five o'clock, though I usually kept the doors open if business was bustling. I suspected I'd be able to close on time, which was a small relief. I had a pack of salmon in the fridge I'd picked up yesterday evening and I planned to smoke it if I could.

I'd recently gotten into watching cooking shows. Figuring out how to cook salmon had always eluded me until recently, though I still hadn't quite perfected the art of it. The health benefits of salmon always convinced me I should be eating more, but it was one of the fishier types of fish. I preferred white fish usually. If you bought it fresh enough, it rarely had that overly fishy taste to it. Salmon was a different story.

Just as I headed over to lock the store up, raised voices alerted me to something going on. I rushed over, only to see Martha Hemming and Betty locked in a heated argument right outside the shop.

I sighed and opened the door. Neither one of them looked at me.

"You ruined my life!" screeched Martha.

Betty waved her hands around. "Leave me alone, you crazy old bat!"

Martha's face grew bright red. She clenched her teeth, and her eyes were wide and angry. "Crazy old bat?" she echoed. "I'm here trying to get you to admit what you did to me!"

Betty tried to shove past me into Tattered Pages. I held my ground. "Absolutely not," I growled. "Neither one of you is coming into my shop until you call a truce."

Martha shifted her gaze to me. "Dakota! How can you be on her side?"

"I'm not on anyone's side. I run a place of business. I don't want any drama or anger brought into Tattered Pages. This place is my livelihood and one I want to protect. So, please. Either make nice or leave."

"You'll be hearing from Mary Ruth about the way you've treated her," Betty warned me.

"Will I now?" I shook my head and was about to turn around to head back inside when a police cruiser pulled up with its lights on. The sirens were off, but red and blue lights whirled around the town square as Hardy pulled up and stepped out of the vehicle.

"Everything okay?" He stepped up behind me and stood there facing down the two women.

Martha dropped her eyes. "I'm just here to try to work this out."

Betty snorted in derision. "Are you? Because it seems like you're only here to attack me."

"Attack you?" Martha hissed in anger. "Every penny of that advance Mary Ruth got is owed to me! You're the one who gave her my book!"

"I did no such thing," Betty said hotly, but her eyes shifted away as she said it.

"I'm going to have to ask both of you to leave." Hardy stepped up closer behind me. "Dakota has already asked, so please don't make this harder than it has to be."

"I'm here to talk to Dakota," Betty said.

"We can talk right here." I didn't want either of them in my shop right now.

"In private," Betty urged.

Martha rolled her eyes. "Why? You trying to steal one of her books so you can give it to Mary Ruth to take credit for?"

Hardy sighed. "Alright, ladies. Let's move it along. Betty, I suggest you try to call Dakota before you show back up here again."

Martha gave me a long look before she turned around and walked away. Betty was a little more resistant. I crossed my arms over my chest and shook my head. "Give me a call. It's more private and I'm about to close up."

Hardy didn't move until Betty stomped away. We watched her climb into her car and leave.

"I don't think this is the last you've heard of her," Hardy said.

"I don't think so either." I held open the door for him to come in. "Did you need something?"

He followed me inside. "No. Trudy gave me a call and

suggested I come by. I was a few blocks over taking care of something, so it was pretty easy to head over before I went back to the station."

"Thanks." I meant it. "Those two shouldn't come within a hundred feet of each other."

"I hope she files a lawsuit. There isn't much I can do about this because it's a civil suit. I can keep them apart as best I can, but other than that..." he shrugged.

"Hopefully they won't be here too much longer. Mary Ruth has one stop here in the state and it was my shop. Binders already had another author booked, so she couldn't go there."

Hardy flopped down into the chair behind the register. He ran a hand through his dark hair and groaned. "Let's hope."

"Rough day?"

Dark circles rested underneath his eyes and his mouth drooped just slightly. He looked more exhausted than I'd ever seen him.

"Rough week," he said. "There's a lot of stuff going on right now with the fallout from Cole's case."

Cole was off the hook, but we'd both inadvertently exposed corruption in town hall and possibly throughout the city. I stayed out of it once I'd proven Cole had nothing to do with the murder. I figured I'd given Hardy enough of a headache with my constant meddling. He could handle the corruption case.

"Sorry," I said, though the words felt inadequate. "Want a cup of coffee?"

He shook his head and stood. "Too late for me. I'll be up all night if I have one now. Thank you, though. I just stopped by to make sure you were okay."

"I'm good." I smiled at him. "Hopefully they don't come back."

He headed over to the door. "Let me know if they do." His gaze lingered on me for a moment. "Have a good evening, Dakota."

"You too, Hardy."

He let the door shut behind him and I watched him all the way to his cruiser.

FOUR

My cell phone rang later that night, just as I was about to get into bed. I groaned and grabbed it from my nightstand.

Cole. "Hello. Everything okay?"

"Everything is fine, but guess what I found out?"

I groaned. "This isn't about Mary Ruth, is it?"

Cole laughed. "Of course it is. This is the scoop of the year!"

"I have no reason to be involved in this," I told him. "And it's late."

"You're going to want to hear this," Cole promised. His voice sobered. "It's not great news."

"Fine. What is it?" I pulled the blankets up and snuggled deeper into the bed. The nights had turned much colder than normal. I had on flannel pajamas and a heavy pair of socks. Knowing me, I'd be up at midnight trying to kick those off, but right now I felt chilled to the bone.

Poppy chose to stay at the shop. I hadn't seen much of her since the Mary Ruth disaster, but she got like that sometimes. Moody and secretive. If she didn't want to be found, she wouldn't.

"The local police reported a body at the same bed-and-breakfast Mary Ruth was staying in. The victim is a redhead."

I sat straight up. "No."

"Scout's honor," Cole said. "It has to be her. I know for a fact that Annie isn't fully booked this week. There's a storm moving in, and people don't want to travel right now."

"Is Hardy at the scene?"

Cole didn't say anything for a moment. "I can only assume he is. Why?"

"He was at the shop today. Trudy called him when Betty and Martha started fighting outside my door."

"You didn't call me?" Cole sounded offended.

"It wasn't scoop worthy."

"I get to decide that, Dakota," Cole sniffed. "Now, tell me, did you kill Mary Ruth?"

I gasped just as Cole's warm laughter rolled over the phone "I'm just kidding."

"You're a terrible person. A woman just died."

"Maybe so," he admitted. "But she is kind of terrible and a liar to boot."

"Doesn't mean she deserved to die."

"Your warm heart will get you eventually," Cole

warned. "Anyhow, I know it's late. I just wanted to tell you. Hardy will probably stop by tomorrow to ask you some questions. It is pretty weird that she wound up dead after Martha accused her of stealing her work."

A horrible thought occurred to me. "Has anyone checked on Martha?"

"Now that I don't know. Seems like if anything, she'd be in custody."

"Martha couldn't have killed her. I've known the woman for a long time. She's no murderer."

"There goes that soft heart again. Mary Ruth stole her life's work. Maybe this was enough to send her over the edge."

I shook my head, even knowing he couldn't see me. "No. She has every right to be angry over it, but she didn't kill Mary Ruth."

"Well," Cole said, his voice thoughtful, "someone did. If the police don't get to the bottom of it, I may."

"I'm not getting involved in this," I swore over the line.

Cole chuckled. "I'd say those are famous last words. Although, if you managed to solve three for three before the police does, I think you're in the wrong line of work."

"Never," I said. I looked over at the clock and grimaced. "I have an early day tomorrow. Talk soon?"

"You betcha," Cole said.

I clicked off the line and stared up at my ceiling for a long time.

Another murder in Silverwood Hollow. It didn't seem real.

. . .

MARTHA HEMMING STOOD outside the door to my shop bright and early the next morning. My hand hesitated on the car door once I pulled up and saw her. Her mouth turned down in a frown when she saw me, and she bowed her head for a moment.

"I'm sorry," she mouthed.

I steeled my shoulders and opened the door. "Hi, Martha."

Her dark hair fell to her shoulders, lank and dull. Her eyes were bloodshot and full of tears. She held out her hands to me.

"I didn't do it," she croaked.

I took her hands. "I know." I gave them a squeeze. "Come on into the store, honey. Do you want a cup of coffee?"

I let her go to unlock the door and then put my arm around her shoulders. She shivered underneath my touch and wouldn't stop. Martha might be in shock. I calmed my racing heart and took her to one of the softer chairs I had.

"Stay here. I'll get you a cup."

She nodded and pulled a tissue out of her bag. A sob bubbled forth from her throat. I hurried over to the coffee pot and used the pod option instead of waiting for a full pot to brew. As soon as the cup was made, I added a little cream and a little sugar and brought it back over to her.

Her cold fingers brushed mine as she accepted the cup. "Thank you." She sniffed and took a shaky sip.

I pulled a chair over and sat down beside her. The store didn't open for another forty-five minutes, and I didn't have much to do any way. Even if I did, all I needed to do was open the register.

I could sit with Martha. She needed a little kindness right now, and I was the closest person who could give it to her.

"Tell me what happened."

She shuddered. "I don't know a lot. But it looks bad for me." Tears fell down her face. Martha and I weren't close enough to share much about our lives, but I knew she was single and didn't have any kids. She came into the store enough to tell me she was an avid reader, and I knew she liked mysteries and sweeter romance. Other than that, Martha Hemming was a mystery to me.

"I found out where she was staying." She chanced a look at me, and I kept my face carefully blank even though I wanted to scream.

"I know," she admitted. "I know it was stupid."

"It's okay. I know how upset you are about what she did."

She drew in a shaky breath. "I knocked on her door and confronted her again about what she did. It turned... ugly. Mary Ruth slapped me."

I blinked and peered closer at her face. Sure enough, there was a small scratch and a bruise forming high on her cheekbone. "She had a ring." Martha pointed to her cheek. "It hurts to talk."

"Did you hit her back?"

Her eyes widened. "No. I swear. When she hit me, I screamed at her. Someone yelled at us and said they were going to call the police." Martha swallowed hard. "I ran off." She sniffed. "I heard this morning that she died."

"Are you sure it's her?"

She nodded. "Betty managed to get my number and called me screaming all kinds of horrible things at me."

"Have you seen Betty?"

"No. I left my house and came here. I wasn't sure what else to do."

It didn't look good for Martha. She had motive and then some, and she might be the last person to see Mary Ruth alive. "Was Betty inside of her room when all of this happened?"

She shook her head. "I didn't see her at all. I think Mary Ruth was the only one there."

"The police are going to be looking for you," I said gently.

She bowed her head and nodded. "I know. I'm so scared, Dakota."

"I know you are." I reached over and squeezed her hand.

She looked up at me, her blue eyes wide and bleak. "Can you help me?"

I blinked. "Help you with what?" My heart sank as I knew what she would say.

"Help me find out who did this?"

"I'm not an investigator, Martha. I really wish I could help, but I can't."

"Of course you can," she insisted. "You helped that one lady out a while back and Cole, too. He tells everyone he sees what you did for him!"

Thanks for that, Cole, I thought. "The police have warned me off any future cases, Martha. I'm really so sorry I can't do more."

She leaned forward, a desperate gleam in her eye. "I'll pay you! I'll... do whatever. Do you need help around here?" She looked around the shop. "Organizing? Cleaning?"

Poppy came out just then and sat down right in front of Martha, her tail swishing back and forth. "Taking care of the cat?" she asked. "I'll do that, but please help me. Even if it's just asking questions." She shook her head. "I don't think I'll be free for long. This all looks very bad for me, so I suspect they'll arrest me. Otherwise, I would. I need help, Dakota. And I know you're good at this."

I swallowed hard. Poppy stared up at me expectantly. And wasn't her timing curious? Hardy would not be pleased with me poking my nose into another one of his investigations. But could I really stand by and watch as they put an innocent woman away?

"I'll try," I said after a moment.

Martha gasped. "You will?"

I nodded. "But I can't get too involved. I'll ask around and see if anyone has seen anything. That's all I can promise."

Martha set her mug down and threw her arms around

me. Her face smashed against my shoulder. "Thank you," she whispered. "Thank you so so much."

Just then, someone knocked on the glass of the shop door. I turned only to see Hardy looming there, a mask of disapproval on his face when he saw who I sat next to.

This was deja vu.

All over again.

FIVE

Hardy didn't say a word to me as he waited for me to unlock the door. As soon as it was open, he brushed past me and headed straight to Martha.

"Miss Hemming, I'm Detective Cavanaugh. I'm going to need you to come down to the station with me for some questions." He gave me a stern look before he continued. "You can choose to come with me, or you can drive your own car, but I'll need you to come in immediately. Do you understand?"

She nodded meekly.

"And, although I shouldn't have to add this, please be advised, the only people authorized to investigate your case are those who've been properly vetted and employed by the Silverwood Hollow Police Department."

Martha's eyes flicked to me.

"So don't rely on any promises made to you by anyone

other than a police officer or someone directly involved in your case. Is that clear?"

I rolled my eyes behind Hardy's back. Martha stared up at him. "Of course."

"Good. Are you ready to go?"

Martha nodded and stood. She followed meekly behind Hardy and when he'd cleared the door, she turned back to me, winked, and mouthed, "thank you" before stepping out of the shop.

I let out a sigh of relief. Hardy would be mad at me for a while, but I really couldn't do anything when someone asked me for my help, could I? I locked the door behind them and hurried up to get the store ready before opening it back up. What a strange start to the morning.

Tattered Pages bustled with customers less than half an hour after opening. I'd given Harper the day off today, so I was way busier than usual. The new paperback releases table was a mess already, so I stepped out from behind the counter to tidy it up. Just as I bent to fix the last book, I overheard two women whispering from behind the romance stacks.

"Did you hear about that author?" one of them whispered. She was tall, blonde, and lean and wore workout gear and a high ponytail.

"Yes," the other one said. This woman was much shorter and curvier. She had long, dark hair in a French braid and wore leggings and a long t-shirt. "Someone said they found her in the room asleep, but when they went to wake her up, they couldn't."

That told me there were no signs of violence. Strange.

"So weird. How old was she?" the blonde asked.

The dark-haired one shrugged. "Not sure, though I don't think too old. Maybe early forties? Too young to die in her sleep, that's for sure."

I fixed the same books over and over as I strained to hear.

"I heard it was poison."

The blonde gasped. "No. In Silverwood Hollow?"

"No one liked her, I guess."

The blonde shook her head. "That's terrible. Can you imagine being so disliked someone slips something in your drink?" She shuddered. "I'd rather someone hit me in the back of the head. Or shoot me. It's much quicker."

"Eww." The dark-haired one looked up at her. "That's kind of morbid."

She laughed. "It's true. With poison you go all foamy and I hear it's pretty painful..."

I drifted away back to the register, my thoughts spinning. Poison? I always read poison was a woman's weapon. But how had she been poisoned? It could only strengthen Martha's case. She had no access to anything Mary Ruth had eaten or drunk.

I blinked as a terrible thought occurred to me. Unless she'd gotten the food from here. I racked my brains trying to remember if she'd taken any food with her when she'd left here so abruptly. Had Betty? I chewed my thumbnail. This would not be good for either of us if she had and that was what had done it.

Trudy and her team set the table up as a serve yourself outfit so anyone could have had access to tamper with the food. But I hadn't heard of anyone else being affected by food poisoning or getting sick after the event, so if the food came from us, they'd targeted Mary Ruth and no one else.

I had to find out her cause of death or see if anyone else had heard those concerning rumors.

When the two women I'd heard gossiping came up to the front with a stack of books, I smiled politely.

"You just missed the signing we had this weekend!" I chirped. "Mary Ruth Steinman was here signing her new book. Are you two fans?"

The women exchanged a look. "You haven't heard?" the dark-haired one asked.

"Heard what?" I kept my voice as innocent as I could make it.

"She died last night," the blonde one said, her voice sounding a little too triumphant for the news she had to share.

I gasped in mock surprise. "Died? How?" I really hoped they had more gossip to share.

The blonde looked over at the dark-haired one. "I heard it was poison. Someone mentioned something about a cupcake wrapper on the nightstand. No real way to know for sure though."

"How terrible," I murmured as I rang them up, my mind spinning with the implications.

A cupcake wrapper.

But probably a muffin wrapper.

I needed to get to Trudy and warn her before the police showed up.

SIX

Trudy's hair was piled on top of her head like she was a country western star. She smiled wide and waved at me as I walked into Sprinkle Heaven.

"Hi, honey!" She breezed over to me and gathered me into a cinnamon spice scented hug.

"Hey Trudy." I hugged her back and spied over her shoulder something I'd never seen before. I pulled back and pointed. "What. Is. That?"

Trudy grinned at me and called to the back. "I knew Dakota would love it!"

"Love what? Spill the beans and give me one, please." I had to sit her down and chat with her about what I'd found out about Mary Ruth, but everyone had time for dessert, right?

She took me by the hand and pulled me over to the display case. Wasn't it sad I knew this case by heart? My poor hips. But... my taste buds were having the time of their life.

"This, my friend, is my newest brainchild."

I steepled my fingers together and wiggled them. "Tell me, mad dessert scientist."

Trudy laughed. "Graham cracker crust. A layer of salted caramel. A layer of milk chocolate." She pointed to a slightly green layer. "Then, roasted, salted pistachios. I bake these together first, let it cool, then pour a layer of crème brûlée on it and bake it again."

I looked at her. "Excuse me. This is crème brûlée?

She made a face. "Sort of?" Trudy laughed. "It's like a souped up odd crème brûlée."

"What's on top of that?"

"Whipped cream, topped with candied pistachios."

"Wow." How did her brain even work? "I'd love one."

"Coming right up, honey." Trudy dished me out a piece and as I paid, I murmured I needed to talk to her.

"Want a cup of coffee with it?"

I nodded.

"Alright. Settle in and I'll bring us both one."

Trudy came over a few minutes later carrying two large steaming mugs. She set one down in front of me.

"What's going on?" she asked as she settled in.

I peered at her. "You've lost weight." It wasn't a question. She'd slimmed way down. "First, I want to ask, are you okay? If you are, then I want to say, you look amazing."

Trudy laughed. "I'm completely fine! I just finally

managed to talk myself out of sampling every single thing I create!"

"How?" I cut into the not crème brûlée thing she hadn't named yet. "I wouldn't be able to resist."

"I hired a young, athletic girl who loves dessert so much she took up running as a hobby so she could keep eating it."

My fork paused in mid-air. "She must really love it because running is the last thing I ever think of when I'm eating dessert."

"She does."

I took a bite of the crème brûlée and moaned it was so good. The salt and sweetness exploded in my mouth. "Trudy. This is..." I shook my head. "The best thing I've ever put in my face."

She snorted.

"I would never, ever tell anyone what you made this with because they'll steal it. This could make you famous."

"Honey, they can have it. I'm too tired to be famous. We opened that second location and all I can do is collapse into bed each night. The reception has been wonderful, but I'm wiped out."

"That's so wonderful." I glanced down at my dessert and my stomach turned as I thought about what I had to tell her. "You should know something."

Her eyes narrowed. "I saw Martha at your shop this morning and I heard about Mary Ruth. What else could there be?"

"People are gossiping about poison."

Her eyes widened for a moment. Then she frowned. A moment later, her face went bone white as the ramifications of that statement hit her.

"No," she whispered.

I nodded. "They found a muffin wrapper on her nightstand. Or at least that's what the rumor mill is saying."

She put her head in her hands. "I'll be ruined."

I reached over and squeezed her arm. "No. I'll do my best to make sure that is never confirmed."

"Did Martha do it?" she asked me, tears swimming in her eyes.

I shook my head. "I don't think so. She asked me to help her."

Trudy brightened. "Of course she did. You're really good at it!"

"No." I snorted. "I'm not. I get lucky most of the time."

"Nonsense," Trudy said, her tone chiding. "You solved three cases in record time."

"I didn't," I insisted, feeling the color warm my face. "I had a lot of help." This conversation felt like deja vu.

"Uh huh." Trudy sipped her coffee. "Martha asked for your help, but I need your help too. Find out what happened. And if you can, make sure no one knows it was my muffins there. No one else has been sick. I definitely would have heard. The investors are talking about opening a third location and I can't risk it."

In for a penny, in for a pound, they say. "I'll do my best, Trudy." I glanced down at my half empty plate. "As long as you keep me supplied in these."

She gave me a dimpled smile. "My pleasure! I'll keep them stocked just for you."

"Deal," I said and dug into the rest of the dessert.

My phone rang just as I closed up shop.

Cole. I huffed a breath and answered the phone.

"Dakota! Martha told me she talked to you today."

"Are we off the record?" I asked as I turned the key in the lock and double checked it was locked.

Cole blew out an annoyed breath. "If we have to be."

I rolled my eyes at his attitude. "You know what I'm going to say here, don't you?"

I could almost hear his annoyance over the line. "Yes," he mimicked me in a high-pitched voice. "Everything I say is off the record."

"Good. And there's your answer."

"So did she talk to you?"

I started the Rav4 and headed back home, clicking my phone over to hands free as I pulled out. "She did."

I grinned as I heard the sound of Cole shifting around on the phone. "And?" he drew the word out.

Laughing, I said, "She knows she's in a tough spot. But she swears she had nothing to do with it."

"And you believe her?"

"I do. She asked me for help."

Cole snorted. "Why wouldn't she? You're almost better than the police force in this town."

I didn't feel comfortable with everyone's vote of confidence. "Maybe so," though I didn't agree with the assessment. "But Hardy is none too pleased with me today. He walked in and found Martha sitting in my shop."

Amusement filled his voice. "I can only imagine. His head probably wanted to explode."

"Not funny," I said even as I chuckled. "It looks bad for her, though. She's the person who saw Mary Ruth last and they had a serious beef with each other."

"I'd say. Stealing someone's book isn't like taking their pen. It can take years to write a good book."

I thought of the knitting chihuahua and refrained from making any comment on the caliber of the book. It was uncharitable at a minimum. People loved that dog and at the end of the day, faith in a series is what moved books.

Cole laughed. "You're judging her!"

He knew me too well. "I am not," I said hotly as I lied through my teeth.

"Oh come on now. I know you like cozy mysteries."

"I do. But I prefer them with fun shops and no magical dogs or cats."

"I don't know," Cole drawled. "That cat of yours seems downright magical sometimes."

She sure did. "She hasn't wanted to come home from the bookstore the last week or so."

Cole seemed surprised by that. "Really? I know she likes to stay there sometimes, but that length seems unusual."

"It does. Ever since we started getting the shop ready for the signing, she's been weird."

Cole and I chatted a little while longer about Poppy,

whether she was eating or acting okay. At the end of the call, we both decided just to keep an eye on her. Cole liked Poppy just as much as I did, even if I wouldn't admit it sometimes.

She'd saved my bacon more than once, so I allowed her eccentricities. Plus, from what I knew about cats, it would be my downfall if I didn't.

Cole and I said our goodbyes just as I pulled into the driveway. When I saw the car sitting in front of my house, my heart sank.

Hardy was here sitting in his patrol car waiting for me.

I wrapped my scarf a little snugger around my neck as I walked up to the car and tapped on the window.

Hardy slid out of the seat with a liquid grace that belied his height.

"Dakota." He nodded.

At least he was still using my first name. "Would you like a cup of hot chocolate?"

Hardy puffed vapor from his mouth and gave me a look almost close to a glare. "I would," he said shortly.

I turned and grinned as I walked up the steps. Few could resist my hot chocolate.

Hardy tugged off his outerwear and hung it on the hook by the door as I did the same. He pulled out a stool at the kitchen bar and watched as I got several things out of the cabinet. When I was a kid, I used to drink the powdered hot chocolate that came in the packages, but when I became an adult and figured out how to make it from scratch, it became one of my favorite things to do during the winter months.

I chopped up unsweetened chocolate and added sugar and some cocoa powder to the pan. I added a tablespoon of water and the chopped chocolate back and turned the heat on low.

He watched me. "No wonder it's so good."

I whisked everything in and made sure there were no lumps in. "It's the only way I drink it now." I tapped the whisk on the side of the pan and put it on the spoon holder before I turned back to him. "Are you here to yell at me?"

His eyes widened. "Should I?"

"You didn't answer my question. You're definitely here to yell at me. Or at minimum, lecture me. You can admit it."

Hardy sat back and studied me. "I'll wait to answer that until the hot chocolate is done."

A laugh bubbled from me. "Fine." Silence fell between us and when the mixture in the pan bubbled, I poured in milk and slowly heated that.

When it finished, I topped the cups off with a little half and half and a touch of vanilla. "Whipped cream?" I asked Hardy.

"Yes, please."

I hid my smile as I got the can out of the fridge. He took his hot chocolate like a little kid would. Just the way I liked mine too. I put a generous dollop on top of his mug and passed it over to him before I did the same to mine.

When I had my fingers cupped around the mug, I took a sip. "Lay it on me."

Hardy held up a finger and took a sip. "Mmm."

"Flattery will get you nowhere," I lectured him.

"Yes, but hopefully it gets me another mug of this."

I waited, one eyebrow raised.

"Fine," he said, though the annoyance on his face was mostly gone now. "You know you can't interfere."

"I am well aware of what I can and can't do in a police investigation."

Hardy rolled his eyes. "Dakota."

"Hardy."

"I'm serious. This is the third time. And I've only been on three murder cases since I arrived in town!"

"I haven't said a word about Martha's case."

"And yet, I found Martha sitting in your shop drinking coffee and crying earlier."

"Everyone needs a friend."

Aggravation flashed in his blue eyes. "I'm advising you to stay out of this. For your own safety and for the safety of the other police officers."

I held my hands up. "It is never my intention to meddle in an investigation. I can't help what people tell me."

"Uh huh," Hardy said, unconvinced. "But you can help what you ask them, can't you?"

He had me there. Though most of my information came through overhearing things. People in this town loved their gossip. I shrugged. "I'm not asking anything anyone else isn't already wondering or asking."

"But you follow through with it." Hardy took another sip of his cocoa.

"Sometimes." I tapped my fingernails on the counter. "But you have to understand, these are my friends."

"I understand it completely which is why I've been patient with you up until now."

I laughed in surprise. "Patient? Is that what you'd call yourself?"

Hardy's eyes darkened. "Considering I could have hauled you off to jail more than once? Yes. I'd say I've been patient."

My mouth fell open. "Jail? For what?!"

"Many things, Dakota. Plus you've had to be rescued more than once."

"I have not!" I said hotly, but when I thought about it, maybe I had. I gave him a considering look. "Those haven't been my fault. Both cases have been close to home and have involved my bookshop."

"Even more reason for you to stay out of things." Hardy sighed and set his mug down. "I'm concerned for your safety and for everyone else's safety. It's a dangerous world out there. Silverwood Hollow used to be safe, but we've had an uptick in crime since I've arrived here. More than anything I want you to be safe."

I shouldn't be annoyed at his statement, but I was. "Last time I checked, I was an adult."

He nodded at that. "You are."

"And as such am responsible for my own safety."

"Yes, you are."

"Alright then."

He slowly shook his head. "Not quite. You are an adult and responsible for your own safety, but other people are allowed to be concerned for you, especially when you make decisions that could endanger you and those around you."

"I've never endangered anyone around me!"

This felt like it was going in the same direction our last argument did. He left my house in a huff and we didn't speak for a while.

Hardy drained his mug and stood to gather up his scarf and jacket. "Thanks for the cocoa, Dakota. You make the best around."

"That's it?"

Hardy's mouth turned down. "Guess so. It's a warning from an officer of the law and concern from a friend. If you don't heed it, then you need to be prepared for the fallout."

Anger filled me, but he'd let himself out before I could speak again.

The nerve of him!

I calmed down around an hour after he left and once I thought about it without being in the moment, I realized he had a point.

I was being a brat. I grabbed my cell, intent on calling him when I decided I should wait until the morning when we were both a little calmer.

His point about me endangering people still rankled,

but I understood where he was coming from. I did have a knack for stumbling into trouble.

I never considered myself a nosy person or someone who involved themselves in other people's affairs, but it sure did seem like I was getting involved a lot when someone got themselves into trouble.

On the other hand, this last time someone asked me to help. The first time directly involved rare books and a customer at my shop, so I felt like I had no choice other than to get involved.

This time, though... should I help Martha out or should I just leave it to the police to solve?

The thought kept me up way longer than I thought it would, and when I woke up the next morning, I felt more than a little bleary-eyed.

SEVEN

I shut the doors at Tattered Pages promptly at one o'clock for an hour lunch. I tried to keep consistent hours, but it really depended on the flow of people. Today had been a steady influx of customers all the way up until 12:45. Harper was off again today, but she'd be in the rest of the week.

Just as I reached to lock the door and turn the sign to *Closed*, Cole came up waving two bags and a drink holder at me. I opened the door up and welcomed him inside.

"Oooh. You brought tacos?"

"Sure did," Cole said as he ducked inside. He set the bags on top of the register desk and pulled out the drinks. "Root beer for you. Tea for me."

"Awesome." I didn't drink a lot of soft drinks, but I had a soft spot for the root beer brewed locally here. There was something about it that reminded me of hot dogs and childhood. "Thanks, Cole."

"My pleasure."

I peeked into the bag and pulled out four tacos. "What did you get?"

"A shrimp and portobello for you and a chicken and brisket for me. They should be labeled."

I doled out the tacos and made room for us over at the seating area. The shop was so quiet when all the customers were gone. The only noise usually ended up being the whir of the air conditioning or heat and the buzzing sound of the lights overhead. I opened the first taco and grinned. "You remembered exactly what I wanted!"

He tapped the side of his head. "It's the skill of a good reporter."

"Well, this is a wonderful surprise. We've missed the last couple of lunch dates."

"We sure did. Life tends to get in the way of social visits sometimes."

Cole and I ate in silence for a little while. When he polished off his first taco, he spoke. "I was thinking about Martha and Mary Ruth. Martha said she gave Betty her manuscript. Do you know how they met each other?"

I chewed on the fried portobello and shook my head.

"Online, I assume," he thought out loud. "I wonder if Betty has some kind of service set up where she exchanges reviews or feedback for a copy of their book."

I really wanted to have a nice lunch and not talk about murder. With Cole, it was almost always about a case he was working or trying to get information about.

"Who knows? Sometimes new writers will trade for

critique, but I don't think Betty is an author. She's a paid assistant for Mary Ruth. Or was, I should say."

Cole's brow furrowed. "I'm trying to figure out why Martha trusted her."

"Who knows?" I sipped my root beer. "Sometimes it's easier to trust people online than it is to trust them in real life."

"Trust, then verify," Cole murmured.

"We aren't all jaded as you are," I remarked.

Cole laughed and opened up his brisket taco. "You learn to be that way in this business. If your sources aren't straight, you don't have a story."

"I wouldn't feel comfortable giving someone my work. It seems weird, but I think it's pretty common. I guess it's a way to bootstrap the process."

Cole's eyebrows went up. "Bootstrap?"

I nodded. "A cheaper way of getting free feedback and some editing without paying for it. Sort of a barter exchange in the writing community."

"You'd think people would use an NDA."

"Some people do, I'm sure. But a lot of these people are new writers looking for help. You don't have to spend any money to send it to an agent, but people are trying to put their best foot forward. Plus, most first novels don't get published."

"Interesting," Cole murmured. "Martha must have written a good book for her to pass it over to Mary Ruth."

"I guess the question is why she would, unless Mary Ruth had purposely asked her to. It seems dangerous, though. Most writers won't look at other people's manuscripts, so they don't get accused of lifting other people's work."

"Maybe Mary Ruth's well had run dry, and she was looking for other ideas."

"Maybe," I said thoughtfully. "Or maybe she never had any ideas of her own. There are rumors out there that she's done this before. Some people on one of the fanfiction sites said she lifted a few of their characters and plot points."

"Brave," Cole mused. "Some people are braver than they should be. From everything I can tell, the writing community is small and things like that always catch up to them."

"They do. There was an interesting case with a pretty big YA author a few years back. You should take a look at that one. A lot of similarities going on in those works. I think it all ended up working out, but those rumors follow her around now. It made me hesitate to buy any of her books for the store, but when I ended up getting multiple requests in a day, I caved. She's still well-loved."

"Mary Ruth isn't," Cole said. "The rumors about her online are savage."

I nodded. "I saw some of them and wondered if I should bring her in." Grimacing at the thought of what happened to her, I shook my head. "Turns out, I shouldn't have. If I said no, she'd probably still be alive."

Cole's mouth turned down. "You can't think like that." He set his taco down and wiped his fingers. "You aren't responsible..." He shut his eyes for a moment and took a breath. "No one is ever responsible for a crime they didn't commit. Thinking like that only invites guilt in."

"I know." I looked away from his concerned gaze. "But ever since I booked that signing, Mary Ruth has been nothing but trouble."

"Trouble does seem to follow her," he agreed. "But it's trouble of her own making."

I couldn't argue with that. Seems like her sins finally caught up with her in a terrible, permanent way.

Cole polished off the rest of his food. His expression turned contemplative. "So. Care to share where you're going to start?"

"Start what?" I muttered through a bite of taco.

"The investigation." I saw right through Cole's nonchalant question.

"Nope. You know what I said. I'm not talking to you about any investigation." Annoyance reared up in me. "Sometimes I think you're only friends with me for the information you think you can get."

Hurt dulled Cole's bright eyes. "Dakota. That's mean."

I shrugged. "It doesn't mean it isn't a little true, though."

With his silence, I knew I was right. I finished up my tacos through the awkward silence and cleaned up the trash. Cole unfolded his tall length from the chair.

We stood there looking at each other. Cole finally spoke. He shoved his hands in his pockets. "It's hard to turn off the job, you know."

"I'm not a source, Cole. I'm a person."

He winced. "I know. It's just I have a job to do and I'm an information gatherer."

"Wherever it comes from."

"Yes. Wherever I can get it."

"Hmm," I said. "Well, you should know by now you won't get it from me. As it is, I've probably shared more than I should."

He gave me an endearing smile. One I'm sure worked on a lot of other women. But not me. "It's this face. It compels you to talk to me." He wiggled his eyebrows.

"No, Cole. It doesn't. I talk to you because you're my friend."

Were? Was? Were we still friends? This felt weird. Like we were burning our bridge together.

"We *are* friends," he insisted.

"I'm your friend."

"Of course!"

"But are you mine, Cole?"

He blinked several times before anger filled his eyes. "I don't know what kind of question that is, Dakota! Of course I'm your friend."

Maybe he was, but was he the kind of friend I needed? He always tried to pump me for information when we were together, even if it was info I didn't have. He rarely, if ever, put down the reins of his job, so I felt hesitant to confide in him.

"Okay," I said after a long moment. "But I think you should sit with that question tonight."

Cole exhaled air, snatched up his tea, and walked out of Tattered Pages.

Two for two in the past twenty-four hours. Bully for me.

POPPY CAME out for a while after lunch and allowed me to pet her. I gave her a good belly and behind the ear scratch before she swatted my hand with a paw. She jumped off the desk and headed back over to the mystery stacks. I watched as she went and just as she slipped around the corner, she turned back to me and yowled.

The last time she acted like this, someone had left a pretty handy clue for me. Feeling weird about it, I followed Poppy into the mystery section. I hadn't been back here since before Mary Ruth's signing, which was unusual for me. My mind had been on other things, though.

She waited for me, her tail raised high, and when she saw me come around the corner, she hopped up onto the fourth shelf. I gasped in surprise, hoping she wouldn't come tumbling back down, but she landed gracefully on all fours.

"Cat, you're going to give me a heart attack," I mumbled.

Poppy yowled and pawed at something. I nudged her out of the way, only to find a cell phone and a small notebook.

"Hmm," I murmured aloud. I picked up the cell and hit the side button. It popped on with 1% battery. The background picture was Mary Ruth and a small, blonde woman I didn't recognize.

I pressed the button, but the password keypad popped up. Someone from the book signing must have left this behind. I flipped through the journal and didn't see anything strange at first.

Then I flipped halfway through and saw some notes about the cat knitting mystery Mary Ruth had just published.

"Oh wow," I whispered.

The woman had written several notes about inconsistencies and small errors within the book, including behavioral quirks with Chihuahuas and how they couldn't possibly knit unless they had opposable thumbs.

That last one made me chuckle in the stacks. Anything was possible with magic. I took the journal and the phone, making sure to give Poppy a good scratch behind the ears, and walked up to the front. The shop was slow right now, so I had time to finish reading if it stayed that way.

But first, because I couldn't help myself, I tried 1234 on the keypad.

It flashed, then opened up.

No way. I stared at the phone, feeling all kinds of conflicted. First of all, holy security issue. Who chose that as their pin code? Second, the home screen had a folder titled "Mary Ruth."

Was this a super fan? I glanced around guiltily and opened it up.

Picture after picture after picture of Mary Ruth filled

the folder. A few documents titled with different versions of *Proof, More Proof* or *More Stolen Work* were scattered in. My hands shook as I opened up one of the Proof folders.

There wasn't much I could decipher, only notes about cats, dogs, magical powers, and knitting. It made no sense to me. I could only assume these were similarities between her books and others.

I looked up only to see Poppy peering at me through the stacks. "Good girl," I said.

She meowed and disappeared.

EIGHT

I stopped by Olive Twist on the way home. Jen, the owner and a friend of mine, called earlier to tell me she had a new blueberry focaccia to die for. I, as a person who cannot resist either blueberries or good bread, hightailed it over to her on the way home.

Jen waved at me as I walked in and stopped short as the smell of garlic and herbs hit me. I loved everything about Silverwood Hollow usually, but this was my favorite thing. How wonderful everything smelled.

"Jen," I breathed as I walked in. "Is it me, or does everything smell even better in here today?"

She grinned at me. "I have a couple of new things, but I knew the blueberry would grab you, so I told you about that one first."

I groaned. "More than one? My poor hips."

She snorted. "Be grateful you don't bake bread for a

living. You have no idea how many miles I have to run to keep the sampling off my hips."

I winced. Running had never been my thing. "Show me what you have, and I'll stop complaining."

She held up a finger. "I'll be right back." Jen rushed to the back, her slim figure disappearing behind a double door.

I looked around the place as she did, surprised to see she'd repainted the walls. They used to be a light brown, but she'd redone them to a pretty light teal. Each table now had fresh flowers in a small vase and a battery-operated candle. Weird. I didn't think she served food, but when I looked up, there was a new menu written in chalk.

She came back out with two plates.

"Jen! I didn't know you opened a cafe."

She set the plates down on a table close to us. "I sure did. I thought I'd surprise you with that as well."

I skimmed the menu and felt my stomach growl. "Everything sounds so delicious." She had all kinds of yummy sandwiches listed, some I'd never heard of. "Raspberry cream cheese brioche sandwich with black forest ham?" I stared at her, open mouthed. "What in the world?"

"It's so good, Dakota. Here, let me get you one!" She rushed off before I could say anything, but I realized I had no dinner plans anyway, so I didn't try too hard to catch her.

The feast before me looked mouthwatering. The blueberry focaccia was warm and golden brown. Some kind of sauce sat in a small bowl next to it. On another small plate rested the other one. I didn't know what it was, but it smelled of roasted garlic and thyme. My fingers itched to dive into it, but I knew I'd better wait for Jen. At least if I didn't want to get judged for my lack of manners.

Jen came back in less than five minutes with a massive sandwich on a plate piled high with kettle cooked chips.

"Wow," I breathed.

Jen handed me a fork and a knife. "Not sure if you need these, but you might for the focaccia." She turned as if to go.

"Jen! Why don't you sit with me? Do you have time?"

Her cheeks colored prettily. "Are you sure?"

I laughed. "Of course I am! You just brought me a mountain of food and I'm dying for the company."

Jen pulled out a chair and sat across from me. She sighed in relief.

"Busy day?" I cut the sandwich in half and nudged half of it over to her.

"Oh, I couldn't!"

"You could and if you're hungry, you should."

Jen chuckled and took half the sandwich. "Today has been a beast. December is always so busy around here."

I'd seen an uptick in business as well, though today had been slower than usual. I could only assume the word about Mary Ruth's murder had gotten out.

"Well, it also helps when you have great reviews and awesome food." I took a bite of the sandwich. Bliss exploded in my mouth. It was the only way to explain it. I wasn't sure what to think when I first saw it on the menu, but everything in it sounded amazing.

Cream cheese on a sandwich. Who would have thought? I chewed and shook my head as I stared at Jen.

"You hate it?" Her face looked stricken.

"No! I love it. This is amazing, Jen! How in the world did you ever come up with it?"

"In the shower," she said with a laugh. "I had the grandkids over for a couple of nights while my daughter and her husband went for a weekend in wine country. They're exhausting by the way, but in a good way." She waved her hand. "Anyway, I finally got them to bed and jumped in the shower, only to realize I was starving. I hadn't eaten all day! To make a long story short, I thought about what I would want to eat, got in the kitchen and made it, then tweaked it a little before I put it on the menu."

"And it's a hit?" I guessed.

She nodded. "Bestseller this week."

"Awesome, Jen. I'm really happy for you."

We chatted about some inane things, and then Mary Ruth was brought up. Jen sighed. "I heard about the author who came to your shop." Her pert nose wrinkled. "I hate to judge, but she sounds terrible."

"She is," I said and winced. "I try to give people the benefit of the doubt, but she was pretty bad even from the beginning."

Jen leaned close. "I heard Martha is a suspect?"

"She is," I whispered, conscious of the people bustling

by us. "Martha stopped by the shop and asked for my help, but I'm hesitant to get involved."

"You're good at getting people to talk. See what you can find out, but be careful. I know you've put yourself in danger a couple of times getting involved with these cases."

"I may start with Betty," I thought out loud.

Her eyes widened. "Betty? Is that the annoying little woman with the inability to stop talking?"

I laughed so hard I gasped for breath. "Yes! I don't know how someone can talk that much and never stop to take a breath!"

Her eyes twinkled with mirth. "She came in here demanding something we didn't have and when we tried to explain it was regional, she went on a fifteen-minute diatribe about why we were wrong!"

I held my stomach. "She's Mary Ruth's assistant. I had to deal with her a lot when the publisher requested the signing at Tattered Pages."

She reached over and patted my hand. "Poor you."

"Well. It could have been worse," I admitted. "I don't often have bad customers at the bookstore, but every once in a while, it can get hairy."

"Maybe you should start with her, then. She's going to be the one who knows the most about Mary Ruth. I cringe to think about all the things my assistants know about me that I don't realize."

"Good thinking." I polished off my half of the sandwich and tried the new focaccia. Both were delicious but the blueberry... "I'll take a whole one of those to go."

Jen's eyes crinkled at the edges. "I knew you'd like it!" She stood to pack it up for me. "Since you're ordering a whole one, I'll throw some extra sauce in the bag."

"Whatever it is, it's delicious."

"It's a basil, balsamic, and olive oil blend."

"Yum." I pushed my plate away. "Thanks, Jen. I appreciate you."

By the time I got back into my car, I had two full bags packed full of Jen's goodies. She'd given me way more than the focaccia and when I realized it and tried to argue, Jen pushed me firmly out the door.

I hesitated to drive over to Betty's with all the stuff in the car, but Jen assured me it would be fine sitting there for a little while. When I pulled up to the B&B, I felt a sense of foreboding well inside of me. Betty wasn't likable, that much was obvious. But did she have something to do with her boss' death?

I climbed out of my Rav4 and headed up to the room. Betty and Mary Ruth had adjoining quarters. The other one next to her was still roped up with police tape. I wouldn't have been surprised if they made her vacate for a little while, but by the looks of it, she was still there. Her tiny smart car sat in the spot right in front of her door.

I jogged up the steps and knocked.

She answered a few moments later, her eyes widening when she saw who stood outside. "Dakota?"

"Hi Betty. I wanted to check in to see how you were doing?"

She wore no makeup and her hair hung lank around

her shoulders. Fine lines touched the edges of her lips, made more pronounced by the frown she wore. She tugged the belt of her robe closer and peered up at me suspiciously. "What do you care? You didn't even like her."

"And how do you know that?" I asked.

"Because you kicked her out!"

I willed myself patience. "I kicked her out because of the scene she and Martha made."

"Martha is a scam artist!"

I didn't know about that. "Maybe. Maybe not. What I do know is they both could have handled it much better than they did. My store is not Mary Ruth's and I have the right to dictate what goes on inside of it."

"She killed her," Betty sniffed, and looked down at her feet.

"I'm not so sure she did. May I come in?"

Betty glared up at me, her eyes welling with unspent tears. She held the door open and stepped away without a word.

I walked inside. The smell of day's old food and unwashed clothes hit me first. My nose wrinkled, but I kept walking.

Betty shoved some clothes out of the way. "You can sit there." She pointed at an old floral chair with wooden armrests. I sat, nervous about the cleanliness of the place, but I knew she was grieving.

"How long are you staying?" I said as she flopped back down on her bed. A pizza box sat in the middle, half empty.

She shrugged. "Not sure. I have to figure out how to transport all these books home. Mary Ruth carried half in her car, and I had half in mine."

"She doesn't have any family that can help?"

Betty snorted. "No one that cares. Mary Ruth burned a lot of bridges." She stared down at her pizza and grimaced. "I'm finding that out now that I'm stuck here in this tiny town."

I bristled at that, but pressed forward. "I'm sure her publisher could help. Have you called them?"

She rolled her eyes. "They're in damage control. Martha has been screaming to everyone who'll listen that Mary Ruth is a thief. They don't want anything to do with her now."

"I'm sure that's not true. Mary Ruth died, Betty. Someone must be around who cared about her."

She looked at me, her eyes red-rimmed from crying. "Me," she said wetly. "I'm the only one."

Oh boy. "I'll ask around and see if anyone can help you get these books back. Maybe the post office can cut you a shipping deal."

She bent her head. "All I wanted was to work in publishing. I never wanted to get involved in all of this."

Sympathy filled me at the statement, but I still wasn't convinced she was innocent. "I want to ask you something, Betty."

She sighed. "Yes, I gave Mary Ruth Martha's book because I thought it showed promise. I never thought she'd lift anything from it."

She said the words I wanted to hear, but her delivery felt flat and unemotional. "How did you and Martha meet?"

"A critique website. Everyone signs up and posts work there for critique. Sometimes you can chat, especially if you like their work."

"And is that what you did?"

Betty shook her head. "No, Martha messaged me. Looking back, I wonder if she found out I worked with Mary Ruth. Maybe she thought she could get closer to her if she knew me." One shoulder lifted and fell. "It wouldn't be the first time someone used me for my connection to her," she said, the words falling from her lips like sour fruit.

"I've known Martha for a while. She seems like a good sort."

Betty snorted. "You still say that, seeing how angry she got?"

"If someone stole something I'd worked hard on, I'd be angry too."

"But now Mary Ruth is dead." She turned and pierced me with her tear-filled eyes. "Would you be that angry?"

"No. Few people would, but I'm not convinced Martha is guilty."

"She's the last one to see her."

"Maybe, maybe not. Where were you?"

Betty scoffed. "Me? You can't be serious!"

"I'm trying to piece together a timeline."

"Yeah, well the police have already asked me all these

questions and I'm not the one in jail, so I think I answered better than Martha did."

"Martha is in jail?"

Her eyes glittered with malice. "She is and I hope she stays there."

I hadn't known. Last time I heard, she'd only been there for questioning. "It still doesn't mean she's guilty. A good friend of mine was arrested recently for something he didn't do. It's the evidence that matters."

"I was out running an errand for Mary Ruth," Betty muttered. "She asked me to go find good internet access so we could find a hotel and get out of this dump."

That rang true. The internet at the B&B was pretty spotty and stayed that way on the road for a while. Too risky to leave and try to find a place while already on the road.

"Did you find anything?"

Betty rolled her eyes. "I'm sitting here, aren't I?"

I prayed for patience. "The book that you gave Mary Ruth. How close is it to Martha's?"

Betty's eyes skittered away. I pressed. "That close?"

"It was almost the entire thing."

I swallowed. "How in the world did she think she'd get away with that?"

"She's a big name in this genre. People forgive a lot of things because they don't want to rock the boat."

"But that's blatant stealing," I protested.

"Don't they call copying the highest form of flattery?"

I scoffed. "That's the worst saying. Stealing is what it is."

"Publishing is full of stealing," Betty shrugged. "Borrowing as well. That's what fanfiction is. Borrowing someone else's characters and making them do things the author would never make them do."

"Martha has every right to be upset," I said gently.

"Maybe so," Betty admitted, "but now Mary Ruth is dead, so I guess she got her revenge, didn't she?"

I sat up straight at that about to press further but someone knocked on the door.

Betty frowned at it but slid off the bed to answer it.

My heart leapt into my throat as I saw who stood outside.

"Miss Adair," Hardy Cavanaugh said, his eyes like stone.

"Detective." I nodded and stood. "I was just leaving."

He grunted. "See that you do."

I glared at him as I tugged my jacket closer around me. I brushed past him and down the stairs. Just as I was about to get into my car, I turned only to see him staring at me, an unreadable look on his face.

I gave him a cheery wave and got into my car.

Well. I didn't get too far with Betty, but what I did figure out is she was lying. About what, I didn't yet know, but I knew deep within that Betty knew more than she let on. And I planned to get to the bottom of it.

NINE

My cell rang about twenty minutes later, but I let it go to voicemail when I saw who was on the other line. I wasn't in the mood to get chewed out by Hardy again.

I stopped by Tattered Pages to check on Poppy. She had plenty of food and room to roam, but it still worried me she didn't want to come home with me.

To my surprise, she stood at the door as soon as I opened it. I bent down, and she leapt right into my arms.

"Hey, you," I cooed. She didn't let me hold her that much, so it felt like a treat when she did.

She meowed at me as if to say, let's go!

I locked the door back and deposited her in the hammock in my back seat. She curled up without a peep and I drove us both home.

My cell rang again, but I didn't even look at it this time. As far as I was concerned, Hardy was out of my thoughts for the rest of the night.

The next morning, I stood at the register ringing up a tourist who'd bought a bundle of romance books - all different kinds to include historical and paranormal.

She practically bounced on her toes as she handed over her card. "I have a whole week away from my husband and kids. They think I'm out living the good life and exploring the state, but I have to confess, I booked a bed-and-breakfast just down the road and I've been ordering room service since I got here!"

"That sounds heavenly." I handed her the card back and bagged her books.

"It is." She sighed. "I love them all, but kids and husbands can be a handful. I needed a break."

"If you ever need a good cup of coffee and a slice of heaven in dessert form, pop next door to Sprinkle Heaven and see my friend, Trudy. She has something in the case that's like a weird crème brûlée, graham cracker pistachio thing that's to die for!"

She gave me a dubious look but laughed anyway. "She hasn't named it?"

"Nope. I suspect because it's too delicious to be named. But you have to try it. If you like all that stuff. She also has some cheesecake that's drool worthy, and her chocolate chip cookies will send you to the moon."

"Well," she said as she gathered up her purchases. "That's quite an endorsement."

"I wouldn't steer you wrong. And if sweets aren't your

thing, try Olive Twist. It's a specialty bread and oil shop, but she just opened a small cafe inside. Try her Raspberry Black Forest Brioche sandwich."

The woman patted her stomach. "I'm going to go home ten pounds heavier."

"Totally worth it," I said.

She waved at me and headed toward the door when the bell jingled. A tall blond man held the door open for her.

"Cole?"

He hurried in, looking around the shop. "Are you the only one here?"

"I am now. Business has slowed since Mary Ruth's death." I frowned. The murder didn't occur here, but people didn't like frequenting shops where murder seemed to be a common theme. Here I was involved in the third one.

He leaned forward and pulled something from his jacket pocket. "Are you sure?" he whispered.

My brows furrowed. "I'm sure."

He didn't seem angry at me anymore, but he was acting weird. Cole pushed the paper toward me. "Take this. It might help you."

I unfolded the sheet of paper and hissed with shock.

"Cole! Where did you get this?" The top of it was stamped with the Silverwood Hollow Police logo.

"It doesn't matter. Write those names down and check into them all."

"What is this?" I said as I scrambled for a pen.

"It's the suspect list for Mary Ruth's murder."

My head jerked up. "Excuse me?"

"Just write them down," he hissed. "Or take a picture or something. Just hurry."

I didn't want any evidence in my cell phone. Peering at the list, I scanned Martha's name, then Betty's, but there were a couple of unfamiliar names on the list. I finally found a pencil in the drawer underneath the register, so I scrawled the names I didn't know on a small notepad I kept close.

When I finished, Cole snatched the paper back up and shoved it into his jacket. Just in time, because the bell rang.

And in came Hardy Cavanaugh.

Cole went deathly pale. I discreetly tucked the paper into my back jean's pocket as he walked in. The air felt stiff with tension and Cole had broken out into a cold sweat.

"Hey Detective," Cole called.

I almost snorted at the awkwardness of it. One of Hardy's eyebrows rose. "Mr. Gardner. Everything okay?"

"Oh, just fine. Everything is fine."

I thought hard about pinching the inside of Cole's arm, but I didn't want him to yelp. Instead, I slid my foot out from the desk and gave him a quick kick on the ankle. Not hard. Just firm enough to warn him to stop being an idiot.

His breath caught, but I saw him visibly force himself to relax. Hardy looked between me and Cole and back again, one eyebrow rising. "Is something going on that I should know about?"

I took pity on Cole. Sort of. "Not at all. Cole was just

relaying the events of his last date with me, and boy was it a stinker. Right, Cole?"

He looked positively green. "Uh yes. She was the worst."

I grinned. "She was. Cole mentioned something about her bathing only once a week in the horse trough down at the Tilly Farm."

Cole's eyes slid to me and widened. My grin grew. "So strange. Apparently, she fancies herself somewhat of a horse whisperer and says that she gets closer to them when she bathes in the water they drink out of."

Hardy's lips pulled back slowly in a horrified grimace before he corrected himself. "Wow," he said politely when he recovered. "That sounds like some date."

Cole stared at me as if I'd grown horns out of my head. "It truly was. Hearing Dakota tell that story was like hearing it for the first time."

I chewed on the side of my lip. "That's why I don't have the timber app or whatever it is. The world is full of weirdos."

"Touché," Cole said. His lips quirked up in a smile, but his eyes promised payback.

"How about you, Hardy?" Cole asked. "Any girls on the hook with you?"

Hardy grunted. "No time for dating. Not interested either."

"Really?" Cole said, his gaze sliding over to me and away before Hardy noticed. "I heard you were the hottest thing in Silverwood Hollow right now."

Hardy's cheeks tinged pink. "I'm sure I'm not." He glanced over at me. I stood frozen, horrified at Cole, but also realizing I kind of deserved this for the horse trough joke.

Cole shook his head. "You have no idea. I even field calls at the office asking me to do a singles column each week. Everyone who asks wants you featured first."

Hardy's eyes narrowed. "Are you messing with me?"

"Absolutely not." He crossed his heart. "I promise. Journalist's honor and all that. The women in this town have a thing for our golden hearted detective."

And with that Cole turned so Hardy couldn't see him, winked at me, and brushed past Hardy on his way out.

Hardy watched him walk out and jerked his thumb over his shoulder as the bell rang announcing Cole's departure. "What in the world was that about?" he demanded.

"No idea," I managed to get out. "But apparently you're quite the hot commodity around here."

Hardy's expression grew annoyed. "I don't care about that." He brushed it away like it had never happened, even as I plotted Cole's murder in my head. "I'm here about Betty."

"What about her?"

"I'm interested in her behavior the day of the signing. Was there anything unusual about her actions that day?"

I thought back to the day of the signing. I hadn't seen anything off from her normal behavior. She chatted too much and was underfoot while we set everything up, but I saw nothing there indicating she might murder someone.

"I don't think so."

Hardy's lips twisted to the side. "Think about every moment you can. When you talked to her. When she sat alone. Anything come to mind?"

"The only thing I can think of is when Martha stood up and accused Mary Ruth of stealing her work. Betty looked extremely uncomfortable, but so did everyone else sitting there. Other than that, I can't really think of anything off."

Hardy hadn't bothered to pull his notebook out for my statement.

"Is everything okay?"

"Yes." His words were clipped. I knew he wouldn't tell me anything anyway, not after our recent fights about my investigating. Not that I'd done too much for this one. Yet.

"Alright then. If there's nothing else I can do for you," I said casually, "then I better get ready for the pre-lunch rush."

Hardy didn't move for a moment and opened his mouth like he wanted to say something but pressed his lips together after a moment and gave me a brief nod before he left the store.

I let out a deep sigh of relief and bent down to fish the piece of paper out that I'd shoved away when Hardy arrived. Harper was due in soon. She'd called earlier asking if she could come in a little bit later. As soon as she did, I planned to go talk to some of these people.

. . .

HARPER BREEZED in looking none the worse for wear. I, on the other hand, felt like I'd been run over by a truck ever since the book signing.

Her blonde hair was swept away from her face and tied up in a becoming messy bun. She wore her favored skinny jeans, flats, white t-shirt, and long cardigan. A pair of new glasses perched on the bridge of her nose giving her a studious air.

She plopped her purse under the desk of the register. "Hey Dakota! Thanks so much for letting me come in a little later today. I'm trying to register for school, and it's been a nightmare."

"Graduate degree?" I inquired. Harper graduated a while ago. I'd given her a bump in pay a little while ago, but I knew she was still underpaid. Or maybe a lot for her skill set. Few people working in a bookshop made big money, but overall Harper seemed happy. I just hoped I didn't lose her. Even as I thought it, I had to laugh at myself. Of course, I'd lose her. She deserved the moon.

"Yes." She stood up and clipped on her name tag. "I'm thinking about Library Science."

"That's a great path," I said. "The librarian here is getting up in age so there might be an opening there soon."

"I heard that. I'm not a hundred percent sure what I want to do yet. I really like working here."

"I'm glad to hear it. I don't think I'll be able to pay you what a Librarian makes, though."

Harper laughed. "Librarians don't make bank either. I

just love books and want to make sure I'm surrounded by them at all times."

"Then you're looking and working in the right career field."

Harper and I worked together for a little while as customers came in and out. The delivery man dropped a huge delivery by the shop which made Harper squee with delight because we'd just gotten in one of the new Nora Roberts' books in.

I left her to tear into those and told her I'd be back in a few hours. She waved me away.

"Just leave me here with all these wonderful books and I won't complain at all." She grinned at me and carefully opened one of the boxes.

"I'll help you catalog this tomorrow."

"Not if I get it done today!" she called.

I laughed as I tugged on my jacket and scarf. With a wave, I left her alone and headed over to see Everett Adams. I'd never met him before and a Google search didn't yield much info other than he appeared to be new to town. He worked in publishing but worked in the next town over remotely. I couldn't tell much more than that, but it did have his home address listed.

Not wanting to be a creeper, I decided to drive past his house and see if I could conveniently bump into him somewhere else. I shivered at the cold blast of air and hurried over to my Rav4. It would take a while for it to heat up and while it did, I could run over to Trudy's shop and grab a cup of coffee.

I breezed in and walked right up to the register. Trudy was nowhere to be found, but a pretty young girl at the register greeted me. "Hi Dakota!"

"Hey Katherine. Trudy around?"

"Not this morning. She's over at the second location." She leaned in and winked. "But Trudy gave me explicit instructions to give you whatever you wanted."

"In that case, I'll take it all," I said with a laugh.

"How about your regular coffee?" she said, chuckling.

"That would be great. A large please with plenty of room for cream and sugar."

"Done." Katherine waved my money away and came back with a steaming cup of coffee. She handed it across. "Trudy wants you to pop back by when you can today. She said she had something to show you."

I held my coffee up in thanks. "I sure will. Have a great day!"

Katherine waved goodbye, and I hurried over to my now warmed up car. I sighed as I slid in. There was something cozy and comforting about a hot cup of coffee and a warm car on a cold winter's day.

Now... to find Everett Adams.

TEN

Candlelight Springs was one town over and had just as much charm as Silverwood Hollow, though I was partial to my town. Where Silverwood was pretty much normal, weird things happened in the other town, sometimes a little supernatural. I suppressed my shudder and kept driving, passing by the small bakery, Binders, and a few other cute little places I'd have to check out once I had more time.

I confirmed the address on my phone map and slowly drove past the small historical home. Just as I went past the driveway, I quickly looked away and sped up a little. A tall man walked down the stairs and got into an old Mazda.

I took a quick turn into a grocery store parking lot that gave me a good view of his car. I'd never followed anyone before, but I wanted to know where he was going so I could casually run into him.

If only my Gran were here. A pang hit me in the chest.

I hadn't seen her nearly enough lately and something like this would be right up her alley. I'd have to call her when I made it back to town.

Everett, or the man I assumed was Everett, pulled out of his driveway and turned the opposite direction. I pulled out behind him keeping at least two car length's distance between us. Candlelight Springs wasn't a large town so hopefully today wasn't the day he decided he needed a road trip. I had stuff to do back at the store later on so I couldn't be out all day.

Thankfully, only a couple of minutes later, Everett turned into the local coffee shop, Beans and Brew. My coffee sat half-finished in the cup holder, so it wasn't a bad thing we were here. I could always grab one of their chai lattes and casually bump into him while I was in there. Conversations always happened in coffee shops.

If I could keep it not awkward, that is.

I waited for Everett to go in, relieved to see he had his laptop with him. That meant he was going to stay awhile. I bundled myself up again and headed inside, scanning the interior of the store to find him.

Everett stood in line, his laptop bag slung over his shoulder. I didn't get a good look at him in his driveway, but now I realized... he was kind of handsome. In a nerdy, bookish sort of way.

His dark hair was on the longish side, but not in a glamorous styled way. More of an *I'm so busy I haven't had time for a haircut* way. A long lock fell rakishly over one eyebrow. He wore gold rimmed wire glasses perched on top of a straight nose. He stared down at his phone, his full lips curved in a frown.

Everett wore light wash jeans, loafers, and a V-neck t-shirt with a trench coat over it and a brightly colored scarf. I stepped up behind him in line. The scent of coffee beans overrode mostly everything else, but when I got closer to him, I smelled citrus and something deeper.

Get it together, Dakota. You aren't here on a date.

Everett looked up and gave me a distracted smile.

"Hi!" I chirped.

"Hey." He looked back down.

"So, have you been here before? I'm from Silverwood Hollow." I jerked a thumb over my shoulder.

He nodded. "Get their chai latte. It's great. You can't go wrong with much here, though."

The barista called for the next person in line and Everett stepped up.

"Nice to meet you!" I called.

He gave me a distracted look and a little wave.

Ugh, Dakota. You are the worst small talker on the planet.

When he finished, he found a booth tucked into the back of the shop. I ordered a chai latte and prayed the table next to him would stay open. How in the world I planned to chat with him when his face was in his laptop, I didn't know. But I'd figure something out.

I paid and rushed over to the table by him as I waited for them to make my drink. Fortunately, I had a notepad in my purse so I took it out so I could look busy. Everett got up to get his drink and I craned my head back to try to get a glimpse of his laptop screen.

No go. He had one of those weird black out things on the screen so you could only see what was on it if you stood directly behind him. Bummer.

He smiled at me as he walked past with his drink. A moment later, they called my name, so I got up to get my drink. As I walked back to the table, a little kid ran right in front of me. I gasped in surprise and tried to pivot only for my ankle to catch on a chair to the side of me.

I wobbled, stumbled, and my coffee flew right out of my hands only to tumble lid over end and fall onto the tile floor, splashing chai everywhere. I held my hands out in front of me to cushion my fall, wondering belatedly if this was the day I broke my wrist, when instead I fell right into a broad, lean chest.

"Ooof," I said.

Two warm arms closed around me.

Oh God. I was crushed against Everett Adams chest. He smelled of lime and pine and I was the perfect height for my head to tuck right under his chin.

I held on for a second only to reestablish my balance. When I had I stepped away, crimson fire burning my cheeks. "I am so, so sorry," I moaned. Chai had spilled everywhere and splashed onto both of our pants.

The kid responsible for the disaster bounded away into the arms of her horrified mother.

"You are in no way responsible for the three-year-old tornado that blew in here," Everett said.

His eyes were honey brown, and he had the smile of a celebrity.

"Erm," I said eloquently.

He still held onto my shoulders. "Are you okay?"

I nodded too quickly. "This. I'm so sorry. Your poor pants."

Everett chuckled, warm and deep.

What the heck is wrong with me? I thought. Everett is a suspect in a murder and I'm over here swooning like a princess in a tower!

The employees rushed over with a bucket and a mop. "I'll make you another latte. Just sit tight."

"That's totally unnecessary," I insisted.

The toddler's mom rushed over. "I am so sorry," she gushed, her eyes giving Everett an appreciative once-over. "Please let me buy your drink."

"It's really fine," I insisted, uncomfortable at all the attention.

The woman turned to Everett. "Oh, you must let me get you another pair of pants!" She touched his arm possessively, and I noticed there was no ring on her finger.

Everett stepped away. "No need to worry. I live right down the road so I can toss them in the wash when I get home."

"Do you now?" the woman purred. "I'm a couple of streets over, too. I'm surprised I've never seen you here."

The little girl in the woman's arms babbled happily to herself. Everett took a step back. "I'm new in town."

"Well then you must want someone to show you

around!" The woman dug in her purse and pulled out a card. "I'm a realtor so I'm very familiar with the area. Give me a call some time."

Everett took the card. "Uh. Okay. Maybe."

The woman gave us a little wave. "See you around then." She left us as the employees mopped up the mess. I finally snapped back to reality.

"Oh, please. You don't have to do that. Why don't you let me clean this up? I'm sure you're busy."

"Not at all," the girl said. "They're bringing you another latte right now."

She finished mopping up the mess and seconds later I had another drink in my hand. I blinked down at it and up at Everett and we both laughed.

"Well, this is certainly an odd way to meet, isn't it?" I said, sticking out my hand. "My name is Dakota. I own Tattered Pages over in Silverwood."

His eyes widened at that. "Ah. The bookstore owner?"

"That's me. And if you've heard of me before right now, I'm very sorry."

His eyes twinkled with amusement. "I have. You're the book-slinging sleuth."

My mouth dropped open. "No," I said with horror. "Please don't tell me that's what they're calling me."

"That's *definitely* what they're calling you." He jerked his head over to his table. "I've been meaning to pop by your store. Want to come sit down and chat with me?"

I stood there stupidly feeling like the tables had suddenly been turned on me. "Erm. Sure. Why not?"

"Great!" He held a hand to my back and guided me to his table.

We sat across from each other. "So," he said after a moment. "Were you looking for me?"

I could start this off with a lie or I could just put it all out on the table. "Yes," I admitted. "Though I did not plan the Toddler Chai Latte apocalypse."

"Very few plans go the way you want them to when a toddler crosses your path." Everett closed his laptop and pushed his notepad away. "What did you want to ask me?"

I frowned, unused to people being so open with me. "Are you sure you're okay with this?"

"Being interrogated by a beautiful, clumsy woman?"

I laughed in spite of myself. "I wouldn't have put it that way, but I suppose yes. Though I hope not to interrogate you. I just wanted to ask a few questions."

He spread his hands wide. "I'm an open book."

Ha. A book metaphor. If Everett wasn't a murder suspect, I might be inclined to like him a little more. A certain detective's face swam in my thoughts for a moment, but I pushed him out.

"You work in publishing?"

He nodded. "I'm an acquiring editor for a mystery publisher."

"Really? How cool! Anything great coming up I need to put on my list?"

One of his eyebrows rose. "Everything I choose is great." He grinned. "But maybe check out the new culinary series we have coming out next year. It's called The Hash Slinging Sleuth."

My nose wrinkled. "Seriously?"

A self-deprecating laugh escaped him. "Seriously. It's really good. Though apparently the title could use some work."

"Do you know Mary Ruth Steinman?"

His smile dropped. "Ah. Yes. She's quite infamous. And I'm not surprised to hear you asking about her. My understanding is she died after a signing at your shop?"

I blew out a breath. "Yes. I had to ask her and another woman to leave the premises."

"Over plagiarism accusations, I hear?"

I nodded. "It got too heated for a small-town bookstore. Plus dealing with her was getting out of hand."

"She's been under an umbrella of rumors ever since she blew onto the scene. I don't know too much about her other than her work has come under scrutiny after her death. It already was, but I'm not sure to what extent. Now that woman..." He tapped his fingers on the table, "Marnie or something?"

"Martha," I corrected.

"Ah. Yes. Martha came forward and sent an email to Mary Ruth's publisher accusing her of taking her work and also implicating Mary Ruth and her agent." He shook his head. "Bad business all around."

I decided to show all my cards. "Do you know why you're on the suspect list?"

A thin smile touched his lips. "First of all, I'm very

curious how you managed to get a copy of that list. Kudos to you." He took a sip of his coffee. "Second, I suppose it's because I went to see her the day she died." Everett snorted. "I shouldn't have. It didn't help the situation any."

"Why did you go see her?"

"You're not going to believe this."

"Try me," I said. "You wouldn't believe the weirdness of my life these days."

"I had a submission come in with a letter that said Mary Ruth had possession of her manuscript and that the woman didn't realize who she was before she researched her online and discovered the accusations of stealing. Normally, I wouldn't blink at something like that, but the manuscript was really good, and Mary Ruth had a cloud of suspicion over her head for that exact thing. I wanted to make sure there wouldn't be any issues with her if I bought the work."

"Let me guess. Mary Ruth didn't take kindly to someone accusing her yet again of stealing?"

"You got it in one. She screamed at me to get out of her room and upheld the lie that she'd never stolen anything in her life." His lip quirked up on one side. "The best part was she screamed at me that everyone was jealous of her."

"Ah. The old jealousy standby."

He raised his cup and tipped it to mine. "The walls started closing in on her and she started unraveling. I've seen it too many times in my line of work. To be honest, I'm not surprised something happened to her, though I never would have guessed murder. She'd done too many people wrong."

"That was the last time you saw her?"

He nodded. "It was. Though I saw Betty that night too."

I perked up at that. "Was she in her room?"

"No. She was here in Candlelight. I saw her getting a coffee here. She had a laptop with her."

"Do you know what time that was?"

Everett's brow furrowed. "Maybe eight or nine? I can't say for sure."

"Did you talk to her?"

"I did. Though not for very long. She saw who I was and tried to pretend she didn't see me. I sat at her table and asked her about Martha's accusations and my client's recent book." He snorted. "She denied everything and said she'd never seen Mary Ruth steal a thing."

"She's loyal. I'll give her that."

"What about Martha?" Everett asked.

"What about her?"

"Don't you think she could have done it?"

"Killed Mary Ruth?" I shrugged. "Maybe. But I don't think so."

"Then who do you think did it?" His eyes glittered with curiosity.

Suddenly, I became very aware that I sat with a murder suspect. Handsome or not, Everett was one of the last people to see Mary Ruth alive. And he had a motive, though a weak one.

"I don't know. I'm not actively involved in the investigation. Martha asked me to ask around."

Everett pulled a sheet of paper from his notepad. "You should look this site up." He scribbled something down and handed it over. "There's a blogger out there who says she worked for Mary Ruth for a while. She has a chronological blog going about the accusations against her and what she saw when she worked there. It's an intriguing read."

I took the sheet of paper and was about to stand when Everett pulled his wallet out and dug around for something.

"And," he said as he handed me a crisp, white card, "when you're done with all of this, you should give me a call." He smiled at me then and I lost my breath. "For dinner. Or so you can spill your latte all over me again."

I took the card even as I felt a hot blush climb over my cheeks. "Uh. Okay."

"Goodbye, Dakota," Everett said.

"Erm. Bye." I turned around and rushed out the door, the card gripped tight in my fingers.

ELEVEN

The meeting with Everett shook me more than I wanted to admit. I drove home a little shaky, a little happy, and a little freaked out. Wasn't Ted Bundy handsome and charismatic?

Relax, I told myself. The odds of him being like Ted Bundy are low.

But I couldn't rule him out as a suspect. And neither could Hardy, apparently.

I drove home without the radio on and tried to get control of my wild thoughts. When I got close to Tattered Pages, I made a detour for Trudy's shop instead of my own. She asked me to stop by and I could use a cookie.

When I came in, Trudy stood at the register.

I rushed up. "Cookie. Please. Stat."

One of her eyebrows rose, but she reached into the case and pulled out two enormous and still warm chocolate chip cookies.

"What in the world? Are you okay?"

I nodded even as I sank my teeth into the chewy yet crispy goodness. "I had a... meeting today with one of the suspects."

Trudy's eyes widened. "Um. Say what?"

I leaned over to whisper to her. "I managed to get a copy of the witness list. His name was on it, and we bumped into each other at a coffee shop in the next town over."

"Bumped into him?" Trudy said, her voice full of disbelief.

"Well," I admitted. "I followed him, but we literally did bump into each other when I tripped over a chair and doused him with my chai latte."

Trudy snorted, then laughed out loud when she realized I was serious. "Sakes alive, Dakota. You're either the luckiest person alive or a walking disaster."

I paused with the cookie in mid-air. "Thanks? I think?"

Trudy waved an impatient hand. "Now tell me. You're all flustered, so one of two things happened. You think he's guilty, or he's ridiculously handsome. Spill it. Which one?"

"Handsome," I blurted. "He's so handsome."

Trudy clapped her hands together in delight.

I held a finger up. "But he's still a murder suspect. I can't ignore that."

"Of course you can't. But... if he's innocent...?" She wiggled her eyebrows.

"He gave me his card."

She gasped. "Best story ever."

Just then, a woman came up and tapped me on the shoulder. I turned.

The woman glanced around and leaned over to me. "Martha said I should come talk to you. My name is Amy."

Trudy waved us away. "I'll bring you both some coffee."

I'd had more coffee and tea today than one woman should stand, but I didn't tell her no. I motioned for the woman to follow me. I picked a booth in the back and made sure her back faced the door. If anyone wanted to see who I was with, they'd have to make a real effort to find out.

She tugged her cardigan closer around her and her eyes darted all over the place. "I saw Mary Ruth. The day of her signing."

I pushed a cookie her way, and she accepted it gratefully. "She was talking to some man. I've never seen him before. But he was big. And he looked angry. I couldn't make out much of what they were saying, but I heard the word 'money' and 'overdue.'"

Trudy dropped off two mugs of steaming coffee. Amy curled her fingers around the mug and inhaled the scent. "She looked scared. I didn't stay around too long after that."

"Could you identify the man if you ever saw him again?"

"Yes. Absolutely. He was on the shorter side. A little paunchy. He had a receding hairline and a big nose."

"Great." I pushed my business card over to her. "I own

the bookshop here. Come on by or give me a call if you remember anything else. Thank you for talking to me."

"Martha. Is she going to be okay?"

I pressed my lips together. "I really hope so."

"I hope so too. She takes care of my daughter sometimes when I can't find a sitter. She's been really good to us."

I reached over and squeezed her fingers. "The police are doing all they can."

"And Martha said so were you." She gave me a short nod and slid out of the booth. "Thank you for the cookie."

"Trudy is the cookie wizard. Thank you again, Amy."

I sat for a while nursing my coffee, lost deep in thought.

As much as I didn't want to, I needed to stop by to see Hardy. He might not appreciate how I got my information, but he might appreciate what I found out.

I cleaned up the mess on my table, gave Trudy a quick hug, and headed back over to Tattered Pages to see if Harper needed anything.

TWELVE

Hardy sat in his office, rubbing his forehead, and muttering under his breath. I stopped at the entrance to his door and my gaze skimmed through his office. He still had the Sherlock Holmes books I'd given him displayed prominently on his shelf. It still made me uncomfortable he had them there considering how much they cost, but he'd told me few people would be brave enough to steal something under his nose at a police station.

There was a mug of coffee sitting in front of him and a half-eaten muffin - one of Trudy's from the look of it.

I knocked on the doorframe. He looked up, his light blue eyes startled. At first, they lit up to see me, then perhaps remembering our last conversation, they darkened and a somewhat thunderous expression took its place.

I stifled my sigh of frustration. "Hi."

"Dakota."

"We don't have to be this way," I said instead of diving right into the case.

"Don't we?" Hardy asked. His brows drew together, and his lips pressed into a thin line.

"No. I'm only helping. That's all."

A deep sigh escaped him. "I don't want to argue about this anymore."

I held my hands up in a gesture of surrender. "Fine. But I do have information for you. Something you may want to hear."

Hardy held my gaze for a long moment, then gestured me inside with a hand motion.

I sat in the uncomfortable chair across from him and was about to speak when a pretty brunette popped her head into the office. "Hey Cavanaugh. Sorry to interrupt, but someone is in the reception area and said they needed to see you. I tried to tell them you were unavailable, but they insisted."

Hardy's jaw clenched, but he stood up. "Stay here," he said. "I'll be right back."

I nodded and clasped my hands together in my lap. "Of course. Take your time."

Hardy left the office, and I looked around the place. The dark furniture and sparse accessories suited him. I looked down at his desk surprised to see how messy it was. Usually everything was stacked neatly in piles and labeled. Today, he had a folder open, its contents spilled out on top, and several piles scattered around. I leaned in, peering at the folder.

Mary Ruth's name was scribbled across the front of it. I looked back out the door. No one was coming. Leaning forward, my heart beating a hundred miles an hour, I peeked at the contents.

A picture of Mary Ruth looked back at me, but it wasn't the woman I grew used to seeing pictures of. This woman had her hair in wild tangles and black mascara circles under her eyes. A mug shot. I nudged the picture out of the way and looked at the info.

Mary Ruth Steinman was listed under the Alias category, along with numerous other names.

Ruth Walters was her real name. I skimmed down the page and gasped as a long list of charges loomed back at me from the paper. Mary Ruth had a rap sheet a mile long!

The first charge listed was embezzlement followed by forgery, theft, and a laundry list of other crimes. Footsteps echoed down the hall, and I quickly nudged the picture back into place and sat back in my chair, making sure I was in the exact same position I'd been in when he left.

Hardy sat back down, noticed what files were out, frowned up at me, and shoved them back in the folder before he spoke. "Sorry about that. What did you need to tell me?"

Although I was curious about who'd pulled his attention away, I felt even more positive about what I'd just found out about Mary Ruth. Or... Ruth Walters. That woman was a real piece of work!

"I just talked with someone at Trudy's who told me

they saw Mary Ruth the day before the signing arguing with a man."

Hardy flipped his notebook open. "Description?"

I relayed what Amy told me. "She said she couldn't make out what they were talking about, but the words 'money' and 'overdue' were mentioned."

Hardy nodded. "Anything else?"

I debated telling him about Everett but decided not to. He hadn't told me a lot and probably nothing Hardy didn't already know. "That's all."

"Thank you for your contribution to this case, Miss Adair." He snapped his notebook shut. "If that's all, I have a lot of work I need to get done today."

I suppressed my hurt feelings over his flippant attitude and kept my face carefully blank. "Of course. I'm always available to help out a *friend*."

Hardy didn't acknowledge my words. A moment later, he dipped his head back down to his work, and I slipped out of his office without another word.

Bummed about his attitude toward me, I called Harper and let her know I'd be heading home. I gave her the option of being paid overtime for a couple of hours or she could go home, and I'd see her tomorrow.

She chose the overtime, and I headed home, trying not to be hurt about Hardy's abrupt dismissal.

Instead of heading home, I made a detour to Cole's work. The place still looked soulless, brown brick, large windows, and still no landscaping. Granted, it was winter now and few people put plants out unless they were cold hardy, but not even a hanging basket with pansies brightened the place up. Maybe I could bring them one later.

The last time I'd been here, I was sneaking around. Today I walked confidently into the building and marched right up to the reception area.

The woman who greeted me looked tired. She pushed her glasses up. "Can I help you?"

"I'm here to see Cole Gardner." I pulled out my license and set it on the desk.

She looked at it and back up at me. "Dakota. You own that bookstore, don't you?"

"That's me." I prayed she wouldn't say anything about a book slinging sleuth.

"I need to stop in and see if you have the new Nora Roberts. I usually order online but I'm trying to get better about shopping local."

"Harper is there today if you wanted to go by. We just got a new shipment in with a ton of the ones you want. Plus, we've expanded our romance offerings too if that's what you're interested in. Not to mention mystery and thrillers and tons of other books." I pushed my card over to her.

She gave me a bright smile. "Cool. Thanks! No wonder Cole talks about you all the time."

My smile slipped a bit, but she didn't notice as she picked up the phone to call him down.

Within less than a minute, Cole appeared at the top of the stairs. He waved and motioned for me to come up.

"This is a pleasant surprise." He looked happy to see me, but a little guarded as well.

"I have a lot of info and a favor to ask."

One of his eyebrows went up. He pressed his index finger to his lips to shh me and motioned for me to come into his office. He'd gotten a promotion since last time. After the disaster with his boss, Liam, and falling under murder suspicion, Cole and I inadvertently exposed a deep source of corruption within the town. Whatever happened afterward had resulted in a nice corner office for Cole, even though the inside of the building was just as drab as the outside of it.

He shut the door behind us and hurried to move a stack of paperwork out of the only other chair. "Have a seat."

I sat down and put my purse in my lap. "No cubicle?"

His eyes crinkled at the sides. "Not anymore. I'm the new Lead Reporter for the Silverwood Hollow Gazette." He flexed a bicep. "It came with a small pay raise and a beige office." He looked around with a wry expression, but I could see the happiness in his eyes.

I knew he'd been promoted, but I hadn't been in his office to see what it led to. "Congratulations. I'm proud of you."

"We both know I couldn't have done it without your help." He perched on the edge of his desk. "Tell me what I can do for you."

"Off the record?" I asked.

Cole's eyes tightened at the edges. "Dakota..."

I stood. "I'm sorry. I shouldn't have come. I know it's difficult for you to separate work and friendship."

"This isn't friendship," Cole said. "You're asking me to help you with a case you know I'm trying to report on and, in the same breath, asking me not to use the information."

He had a point. I squirmed uncomfortably. "What information do you have?"

Cole snorted. "And why would I tell you?"

Exasperated, I looked up at the ceiling. "I'm trying not to get entangled up in this too much and I don't want to be called to the stand as a source!"

"We protect our sources. At all costs." Cole leaned forward, his hands clasped together in his lap. "Help me and I'll help you."

At that moment, I knew Cole and I were never destined for more. Our relationship flipped in an odd way. I became a tool to him and sitting here looking at him, seeing the desperate gleam in his eyes for a scoop, I decided he needed to become the same to me.

"Fine. I want complete anonymity. And I won't share everything. Plus, you tell me what you know first so I don't repeat something."

Cole's lips quirked up in an odd sort of smile and sadness filled his eyes. He knew it too.

"I have the witness list and a report that Everett was one of the last people to see Mary Ruth alive the same day she was murdered."

I nodded. "He was. A woman named Amy saw her the day before the signing."

His eyes lit up at that. "She said she saw her arguing with a man - someone she didn't recognize. They argued about money, and she said Mary Ruth looked really scared."

Cole reached over for a notepad and scrawled something down. "Do you know what he looked like?"

I told him what Amy had told me. Thinking about what else I knew, I sorted through the pieces of info to see if I had anything else to give him. The tidbit about the muffin wrapper would stay with me. I promised Trudy and so far it hadn't gotten out. I planned to keep it that way.

"Do you know how Mary Ruth died?"

He nodded slowly. "Looks like poison. Though I haven't been able to determine what kind."

"So she died slowly?"

He shook his head. "No idea. It depends on what kind of poison was used. Sometimes it takes a person quickly. Sometimes the death can be agonizing. But there was no indication she died slowly. So that's something in the good category." He paused. "If there's anything positive about this case at all."

I definitely wasn't telling him about the muffin wrapper then. I gave him a couple more tidbits, then sprung what I needed on him.

When he learned Mary Ruth's real name, his eyebrows went up to his hairline. "This is great stuff, Dakota."

I pressed down the tears threatening to spring from my eyes and cleared my throat. "Sure, Cole. I need to know as much as possible about Ruth Walters. If we can figure out who she was in real life, maybe we can figure out who wanted to harm her."

He clicked his pen off and set his notebook aside. "I'll do my best. Now that I know her real name, it should be pretty easy to dig into her background." He scratched the five o'clock shadow forming on his cheeks. "This changes things, doesn't it?"

"I'm afraid so."

Cole nodded. Silence fell between us. Awkward this time when it never had before. I stood up and put my purse strap over my shoulder. "Well, please let me know what you find out. After this, we're square. Right?"

A sad smile touched his lips. "Square. If that's what you want to call it, Dakota."

I nodded and opened the door to his office, not daring to let my eyes leak until I got back into my car and drove home.

THIRTEEN

The next morning turned dark and dreary in a hurry. I dressed as warm as I could and put on makeup and tried to somewhat fix my hair. It wouldn't matter so much when I put my winter hat on, but at least I tried. I had another woman on the suspect list I wanted to talk to this morning, but I also needed to get to the shop to help Harper with the new inventory. Getting an early start was ideal today.

I headed over to the town on the other side of Silverwood Hollow, opposite of Candlelight Springs. I rarely came into Harmony Bay, but Autumn, the other woman on the list, had a bay home right on the water.

I drove for about twenty minutes until I pulled up in front of a two story pretty blue house. I would have rather met her in public, but after the chai disaster, I decided just to knock on the door and see what happened.

I tugged my hat down over my hair and readjusted my

scarf before I jogged up the steps and knocked on her door. A pretty older woman answered.

She looked to be in her early fifties with light blonde hair and a pair of red glasses perched on top of her head. For some reason, she looked really familiar to me...

She smiled at me politely but didn't open the screen portion of her door. "Can I help you?"

"Yes, ma'am. My name is Dakota Adair. I live in Silverwood Hollow. I wanted to ask you some questions about Mary Ruth Steinman."

Her expression shut down immediately, all pretense of friendliness wiped from her face. "What about her?" she asked flatly.

"Well, I know you know her, and I was wondering if it had to do with something you might have written?" I'd been thinking about it and if this woman was on the suspect list, then she either was an author or had something to do with publishing. It just made sense.

The woman's eyes were flat. "I'm not sure who you are, but I don't have to answer any of your questions." She started to shut the door, but I held out a hand.

"Please, wait. I'm just a bookstore owner, I promise. I'm here because a friend of mine is a suspect, and she swears to me she didn't do it."

The door paused in her hand. "A suspect? For what?"

I blinked. "You haven't heard?"

She shook her head. "Heard what?"

"Mary Ruth was murdered a few days ago."

The woman's eyes widened. For a second, she stood

there stunned. Finally, she held the door open. "It's cold outside. Why don't you come in?"

I thanked her and followed her inside where it was warm and toasty. "I'm Autumn, by the way," she said as she led me inside to the living room.

I knew her name, but I was glad she introduced herself.

"Would you like a cup of tea? I'm afraid I don't drink coffee."

"I'd love one."

"Please have a seat."

I settled in on a comfortable blue couch and waited for her to bring refreshments. Her house was tidy and well kept. Only a few photos sat on a large bookshelf. Her with a group of friends and a large family photo. Autumn didn't seem like she was married or had children.

A piano sat tucked into a corner, free of dust, which told me it was well used. Books were stacked haphazardly on top of a table along with a laptop and a notepad with several pens scattered around. On the bookshelf, there were classics and modern fiction - a selection of romance, mysteries, and fantasy. I'd have to invite her to Tattered Pages if she ever got out to Silverwood Hollow.

A few minutes later, Autumn came back in with a silver tea pot, two pretty China cups, and a bowl of sugar and cream. "Wow," I said with a laugh. "This is a real tea service."

She smiled and poured a cup. The fragrant scent of bergamot drifted out. "I hope you don't mind Earl Grey."

"It's one of my favorites." We doctored up our drinks and chatted amiably for a bit before Autumn set her cup down.

"I can't believe she's gone. I waited years for her to pay for what she did to me and now I'll never see it."

"May I ask what she did? I suspect you're either a writer or in the publishing business. Mary Ruth has left some shrapnel behind, that's for sure. She seems to have a reputation for lifting other people's work."

Autumn snorted with disgust. "That's a very nice way of saying that woman is a raging thief. We used to be in a writer's group together many years ago. She's the kind of person you warm up to fast because she knows how to play you." Autumn shook her head. "I fell for it hook, line, and sinker. We became critique partners, and everything was fine until I noticed she was taking a lot more work of mine than I was of hers. I didn't think much of it at first. After all, a lot of people in writing groups don't write that much. They just talk about writing." She laughed. "But Ruth had big dreams of fame and she kept talking about a project she was shopping around."

I noticed she said Ruth and not Mary Ruth. "You know her as Ruth and not Mary Ruth?"

"Oh yes," Autumn said. "She's taken many pen names over the years to try and escape what she's done."

"Yeesh," I murmured.

"It wasn't until she left the critique group and stopped returning my calls that I got really suspicious. Six months later, I saw a social media post go up about the book she sold to a major publishing house."

"Let me guess," I said dryly. "The book was yours?"

"Right down to the cleft in the handsome detective's chin."

"I'm so sorry."

She sighed. "Hindsight is always twenty twenty, you know? There wasn't a thing I could do about it, either. I talked to a lawyer and everything. She said since we were swapping writing, there was no real way to prove the work was mine. And even if I could, those cases are prohibitively expensive to take to court. It would bankrupt me trying to fight her."

"She did it to my friend, too. That's why I'm here."

Autumn laughed, a sad, bitter sound. "Honey, she's done it to more than me and your friend. There's a string of people around this area she's stolen from. And when she's about to get caught, she resurfaces somewhere else with a new pen name but that same old rotten face."

Autumn took another sip of her tea. "What made it even worse was that I sold my book right during the time she was also selling it. It was my debut, but Ruth got the news out first and my publisher cancelled the publication. I had to return my advance and everything."

I gasped in surprise. "That's horrible."

"It is. And no matter what I told them; it didn't change anything." She glanced over at the table. "I still write, but I'm terrified to try to sell my work again. And I never, ever tell anyone what I'm working on anymore."

Grief filled me at her words. She'd worked so hard on something only to have it ripped away from her. "If you ever sell anything, please reach out to me. I'd love to have you at my shop."

"That's awful nice of you. I just don't know when I'll be ready again."

"Understandable." This didn't clear Autumn from suspicion. In fact, it made her even more of a suspect, but the woman in front of me didn't seem like a murderer.

"Harmony Sussex is the name she used when she published that book. It's still in print." A bitter laugh escaped her. "I buy copies just to set them on fire."

I'm sure she knew Mary Ruth got royalties from them anyway. It probably made her feel better to see them in ashes.

"Thank you for talking to me today." I put a card on the table. "If you're ever in town, please stop by. We can have a cup of coffee and catch up."

"Please keep me informed about the investigation?"

"As much as I can." I stood up and showed myself out.

How many lives had Mary Ruth ruined?

Any sympathy I felt for the woman fell away as I drove back to town. No one deserved to die, but she'd deserved something for all the pain she caused. A few minutes after I drove away, I realized why she looked familiar. The cell phone I found belonged to her. I'd find a way to get it back to her later. She must have shown up to the signing. To what end, I didn't know.

. . .

IT WAS close to lunch time before I made it back to Silverwood Hollow, so I stopped in and grabbed a sandwich at a local deli before heading back to the store. I ate in the car and was just taking my last sip of water when I walked in.

Harper had boxes piled high against the back wall and was slowly checking them off of the spreadsheet I'd made with all the new books I ordered.

I marched up to her and gestured for her to hand me the spreadsheet. "Take a long lunch. I got this for a while."

Harper stood and stretched her back out. "Thank you so much. I'm glad you're back. My realtor called and has a house to show me just a few blocks down. Mind if I take a peek during my break?"

My face lit up. "Here?"

Harper laughed. "Yep. One finally came on the market that checked most of my boxes."

"Sure! Take your time!"

Harper waved and headed out the door, grabbing her jacket and scarf on the way.

Poppy came out just then for some attention. I scratched the back of her neck. "Want to come home tonight?"

She meowed at me and disappeared back into the stacks. "Darn cat," I said with a laugh.

I checked out one customer who'd come in for a new thriller we'd just got in and someone else came in a while later looking for a copy of an old Shakespeare book we used to have.

"Sorry, we just sold that one a few days ago."

"Bummer," the girl said. "Is there any way to order another?"

"Maybe," I hedged. "I'll have to see if I can find one. Leave your name and number and I can give you a call if I find it."

She happily did so and left the shop waving as she did. With no other customers, I went back to checking the inventory and got so absorbed in it, when I finally got out of my seated position, my back screamed with agony.

I glanced at the clock and realized I'd spent a good two hours on the floor without a single customer. Concern lurched in my stomach over it. By now, I usually had a good rush of people.

Trying not to panic, I forced myself to take several deep breaths. Harriet from Binders was just now getting her customers back. It took her a while to overcome people's fear after someone had found a body in the parking lot. Maybe this was the same thing.

Except... no one was killed here. However, I was associated with it.

Again.

Harper breezed back in shortly after, her eyes sparkling with happiness. "It's wonderful, Dakota! I put an offer in."

I gasped with surprise. "You did?"

"I did. It's affordable and Mom and Dad are helping

out with the down payment."

I beamed with pride at her. "That's wonderful news! Why don't you take the rest of the day off?"

She laughed, a happy sound. "I can't! I just bought a house!"

"Well then," I said as I handed over part of the spreadsheet. "Better get to work then."

RIGHT BEFORE CLOSING, a woman came into the shop looking around, her eyes pinched and her mouth tight. She looked unfriendly and not in the mood to chat.

"Hello," I said. "I'm Dakota. Welcome to Tattered Pages. Can I help you find something?"

The woman stripped off her gloves. "I'm Maria Fontenot, Mary Ruth's agent. I'm here to pick up the books she left behind."

My eyebrows rose. Was this normal? "Um. I expected her publisher to send a representative?"

Maria sniffed and handed me a folded note. "Here. I'm designated as a rep from them. She has no one else to do it for her and the publisher is too far away. They're shorthanded right now."

I skimmed over the note and tucked it into my pocket. This entire situation was odd. "If you'll follow me to the back, I can get those for you."

Maria nodded, her gaze skimming over the shelves. From the look on her face, she wasn't impressed.

I led her to the back and opened up the office. Several

boxes with the publisher's stamp sat on top of a vacant desk. "They're right here. Do you have someone to help you carry them out?"

"You?" Maria said hopefully.

"I can help, but I warn you, these are heavy boxes. We may need to work together."

Maria eyed the boxes and sighed. "I don't even know why I'm here," she muttered. "This is not my job."

"How well did you know Mary Ruth?" I asked nonchalantly.

Her eyes flicked back to me. "Well enough, I suppose. I don't make friends with my authors. It's a business transaction for me."

I opened my mouth to say something, but Maria interrupted me. "I've heard about you. You fancy yourself as some kind of sleuth, right?"

"Not quite," I said, forcing myself to be polite.

"Well, you can ask all you want, but I had nothing to do with those allegations against Mary Ruth."

"Martha Hemming said she sent you her work. The same work Mary Ruth stole."

Her lips tightened, and she looked away but not before I saw anger flash in her eyes. "Martha is a liar," she hissed. She hefted one side of one of the boxes up. "Help me with this."

I lifted the other side, and we slowly walked through the store. "So you're saying Martha lied about sending her work to you?"

"I'm not saying anything else to you," she snapped as

we loaded the box into the back of her SUV.

"What does it matter?" I ask. "Mary Ruth is gone now and Martha is under suspicion for murder."

Maria stomped back inside for another box. "It matters because my reputation is at stake and you're a complete, nosy stranger to me."

I blinked at her venom and helped her with another box. "If you don't have any culpability in this, I don't see why you wouldn't deny it to save yourself."

"Oh shut up," she snapped as we put the second box in. "Someone like you wouldn't understand the pressure someone like me is under."

I tilted my head. "Oh?"

She went pale as she realized what she said. "Just help me with these so I can get out of here."

Maria refused to say another word as we loaded the rest of the boxes up. I held the door open for her as she snatched her purse up, but just as she walked out, I noticed Hardy jogging up the sidewalk. I started to close the door, but he barked out, "Don't go anywhere!"

Sighing, I stood there outside, freezing, as Hardy cornered Maria. He walked her around the side of her car so I couldn't hear or see them. When he finished talking to her, she slammed the door and roared off.

Hardy crossed his arms and gave me a look. "What?" I snapped. "She came here to get the books Mary Ruth left behind."

"I know."

"Then why do you look so annoyed?"

"Because you tried pumping her for info, didn't you?"

"So what if I did?" I asked hotly.

He took two large strides until he was in my personal space and loomed over me. "You're going to get hurt if you keep putting your nose where it doesn't belong. And I am not always going to be here to save you."

"You have a Prince Charming complex," I blurted.

His gaze narrowed. "Excuse me?"

"He came in with a hero complex but didn't even remember what Cinderella looked like, then sent a minion with a shoe across the kingdom to solve the mystery!"

"I - I have no idea what that means," he said, his voice baffled.

"It means you want to solve the case, but you don't do the necessary work!"

Hardy's face went thunderous.

I stepped back, immediately regretting my words. "Oh. Oh, Hardy. I didn't mean that at all. I promise."

When he spoke again, it was slow and measured. "You have no idea the kind of work done behind the scenes I do. Investigations are slow and measured things, not romantically dumping your chai latte and falling into a suspect's arms!"

I blinked at him.

"Yes, Dakota. I'm well aware of your little meeting with Everett Adams. I wouldn't forget he's a suspect in the murder of Mary Ruth Steinman. He might have a pretty face, but he could very well be dangerous."

"I'm well aware of that," I snapped.

"People trust you," Hardy observed. "It's annoying."

"I have a good track record," I insisted. "They know they can trust me."

Hardy pointed to the newspaper display across the street. "Can they, Dakota?"

With that, he tipped an imaginary hat at me and walked away.

Horror filled me. I rushed across the street and bought a Gazette.

On the first page, a large picture of Mary Ruth glared back at me with the headline, *Fraudster Exposed!* Underneath the picture were the words, "A small town favorite spills the tea and gives an update on the investigation!"

Oh, Cole.

Dejected, I headed back to the bookstore, leaving my friendship with Cole broken behind me.

FOURTEEN

Harper stood at the door waiting for me. She held a letter in her hand. Her eyes were wide, and her fingers trembled as she handed it over.

"Harper?"

"You need to read this."

I took the letter and skimmed the contents. The handwriting was small and spidery, forcing me to squint as I read. Once I got to the bottom, I looked up at Harper.

"This is bad, right?" she asked, her face pale.

"Very. I'm going to have to turn this over to Hardy."

Harper's gaze went up and her eyes widened. "Letter," she barked.

Without knowing who was behind me, I shoved it into my jacket.

The bell rang and Cole walked in.

His gaze bounced between us both, but he didn't ask us

what was going on. Good thing too. I didn't feel so friendly toward Cole right now.

"Hey, I wanted to come by and talk to you before you saw -"

I held the newspaper up. "This?"

He dipped his head. "That."

"You protect your sources at all costs, do you?" I asked, using air quotes for the word protect.

His lips thinned. "It's what the boss wanted."

"At the cost of our relationship?"

Harper took a couple of steps back and hurried away from us, probably not wanting to get caught in the crossfire.

"I had no choice."

"You did have a choice," I said. "I sat there and told you what I knew and trusted you to keep me a secret. Now the entire town thinks I'm out there blabbing to you about Mary Ruth's murder! Hardy is furious with me!"

"Oh come off it, Dakota. When is Hardy *not* furious with you?"

"Don't deflect this onto him. You and I had an agreement, and you broke it."

"I couldn't help it."

"You could." I insisted. "But the story was more important to you."

I walked up and held the door open. "I want you to leave."

Cole shoved his hands in his pockets, his face stricken. "Dakota, I -"

I didn't want to hear it. I pointed outside. "Please go."

Cole brushed past me without another word. When the bell dinged again, Harper peeked her head out of the back.

"Coast clear?"

"For now," I said.

"Cole. Wow. That's messed up." Harper peered out the door as Cole walked away. "He looks devastated."

"Well, he should. He betrayed my confidence in a pretty big way."

Harper pressed her lips together. "Do you think he had to?"

"No one has to do anything." I rubbed my eyes. "I rarely told him anything because of this exact thing and the one time I do, he reveals me to everyone!"

Harper leaned against the door, her face thoughtful. "He must have been put in a pretty tight spot to do this because everyone can see how much he cares about you."

"Well," I said as I pulled my jacket off, "he cares about his job more, though. And isn't that the problem?"

HARPER AND I worked mostly in silence for the rest of the day. She left before me, and I worked to finish up the inventory. Christmas was almost here, and we'd been so busy I had to make an entirely new order, so these were extra. Now that they were all out on display, though, I wondered if I had made a mistake, especially with the shop being slow right when it should be at its peak.

I brushed those maudlin thoughts off and started to

lock up, calling for Poppy who stared at me from the romance section, her yellow-green eyes glowing in the dim light.

"Want to come?"

She put her tail up and walked away. I chuckled and double checked the locks before I headed out.

A hot chocolate sounded divine, so I popped over to Trudy's. Hoping I could resist dessert (even though hot chocolate is a dessert!), I made my way up to the register.

"Hey Dakota! Hot chocolate?"

"Just what I need." Trudy rarely offered me coffee in the afternoon unless I looked rough. Usually, it was tea or hot chocolate and today was definitely a chocolate kind of day. Her eyes were kind as she pressed the cup into my hand and waved away my money.

"I saw the newspaper today," she said.

I looked down at my cup. "Yep," was all I could say.

"I'm so sorry, honey."

"Me too," someone said from behind. I turned and saw Martha standing there, fury written all over her face.

Trudy took a step back and grimaced. "I'll leave you two alone."

"Would you like to get a table?" I asked, steeling myself for the inevitable conversation ahead of us.

She sailed in front of me and plopped into a chair. "You were supposed to keep this on the down low," she hissed as soon as I sat down.

"I needed something from Cole, and he needed something from me. Though he wasn't supposed to do what he did."

"What he did was blast my business all over the town and paint you as some kind of Investigative Dear Abby! I just got out on bail and I'm not so inclined to go right back!"

"I'm well aware," I said wryly. "On another note, I received a disturbing letter today."

"Oh?"

"From someone who claims you led a smear campaign against Mary Ruth."

Her eyes narrowed. "She got into my reading group under a false name and started stealing ideas from the readers and writers in there! The nerve of that woman!"

"So you decided to ruin her life?"

"Just like she ruined mine?" she snapped. "Yes, I did. And it worked too. Somewhat," she amended.

"You got her kicked off social media?"

Martha's smile turned nasty. "I did, so she had the brat Betty do the posting for her."

"What were you trying to do?"

"I was trying to prevent her from ever doing something like that again!"

"It was too late for you, though?"

"Yes. Her debut had already been released. She managed to hush this up and I still don't know how." Bitterness and anger dripped from Martha's voice.

"It doesn't matter anymore," I said.

"Of course it does. She still got that money and I got nothing!"

This Martha... I didn't know this Martha. She sounded like a woman who could kill someone if she got angry enough. I didn't like it.

Martha pinched the space between her brows. "Look, Dakota. I'm counting on you. I need some evidence that points to someone else." She leaned in closer. "I heard her agent is in town. Have you seen her yet?"

I tilted my head. "Where did you hear that?"

She waved away my concerns. "Small town America. Did you talk to her?"

I nodded slowly. "But I didn't get anything out of her."

She slapped the table, jarring the sugar container. I leaned back, away from her anger.

"I'm sorry," she whispered. "I just know I'm not going to be off the hook for long. I've been lucky, but I feel like they're closing in on me."

"I'm doing the best I can. You know I'm not a professional investigator."

"Of course I know that. I don't know what the police department is doing right now."

"Everything they can," I assured her.

She shook her head and stood. Her arms wrapped around her chest, and she shivered. "I didn't do it. I swear to you. No matter what the people in this town think."

Martha left me sitting there alone, my hot chocolate rapidly cooling. My thoughts spun as I tried to figure out who would have done something like this to Mary Ruth when so many people wanted her punished.

I tossed a tip down on the table for Trudy and waved to her as I left the shop. As I walked to my car, I noticed something stuck in the windshield wipers. When I got closer, I realized it was a manila envelope. I looked around but didn't see anyone, so I took it off and got into the car.

I'd look at it when I got home.

CURLED up on my couch with a glass of wine and the television playing quietly in the background, I opened the envelope and tipped the contents out. A paper clipped short stack of papers and some pictures spilled out along with a short handwritten note from Cole.

This is all I could find. I'm sorry it turned out this way - Cole

I put the note aside and flipped through the papers he'd sent me. Turned out Ruth Walters hadn't been a good person since her youth. Cole had scoured research databases and websites and found at least two other people Mary Ruth had stolen from. Not only that, but she'd also somehow managed to get a new social security number and duped a new publisher into taking her on with a new pen name. This could clear the publisher of any wrongdoing. With her new social, anything on Ruth or any criminal checks would come up clear.

She'd been a smart, manipulative woman.

My cellphone rang a little while later. "Hey honey,"

Trudy said when I picked up. "Just wanted to let you know your little nugget is yowling at the door."

"Of course she is," I said wryly. I'd just gotten into my pajamas too. "I'll go get her."

"Alrighty then. She's yelling up a storm. That's one weird cat, Dakota."

"Don't I know it." We hung up, and I dressed quickly before grabbing the keys and heading out. I suspected Poppy knew exactly how much it annoyed me when she did this, which is probably why she did it.

It took only a few minutes to get to the store. I unlocked the door and Poppy jumped right into my arms. Depositing her into the hammock in the back, I climbed back into the driver's seat and glared at her through the rearview.

"I'd just poured a glass of wine and had my pajamas on. What did I ever do to you?"

Poppy stared at me with wide eyes before she looked away and took to grooming herself.

I snorted and pulled away from the store. Sprinkle Heaven was closed up tight as were most of the shops in the square. The town looked gorgeous right now, all lit up with clear and twinkling lights, red and green ribbon wrapped around the light poles and garlands everywhere.

A sense of warmth filled me as I drove slowly through town. I didn't have anyone special with me this year and that was okay. I had a grumpy cat in the backseat and Trudy and Jen. Plus, Mom and Gran and kooky Aunt Corky. It was enough for now.

I was only about a mile from the house and slowly pulling away from downtown when a woman darted out right in front of my car. I slammed on the brakes, my heart beating wildly.

"What in the world?" I said out loud.

Poppy let out a god-awful screeching whine. I looked back at her and then back at the woman, but she was gone.

"Poppy?"

She abruptly stopped but stared in the direction the woman had gone. Getting out of my car seemed like a dangerous proposition, but that woman could be in trouble.

"What do you think?" I asked the cat.

Poppy meowed at a much more normal level this time. "Should I follow her?"

She meowed again. I got my cellphone out and dialed Hardy. Surprise, surprise, he didn't pick up.

As I got out of the car, I left him a rambling message about where I was and what had happened, then told him I was going to see if I could find her.

I could just see his head explode over that one.

"Stay here, Poppy." The cat didn't move an inch.

"Sure," I grumbled, "let me get out in the frigid winter so you can keep your toes toasty. I get it."

I shut the car door and walked in the direction the woman fled. "Hello?" I called into the dark. Downtown was behind me. Ahead of me was a lot of trees and dense forestry. "It's really cold out here. Do you need a ride?"

No answer. I looked back at my car and chewed on my

thumbnail. This was dangerous. Hardy's words came back to me. I blew out an indecisive breath and took a few more steps forward. I called out again but heard nothing in return. I couldn't see very far in front of me and what I did see was only trees.

I turned around to head back to the car and had taken just a couple of steps when pain burst in the back of my head. I fell to my knees, the headlights of my car blurring in my vision when I slumped forward, my eyes unable to stay open.

FIFTEEN

An urgent voice broke through the fog in my head. "Dakota?"

I stirred. "Dakota!"

Gentle hands held my head. "Don't move. An ambulance is on the way."

I shook my head and groaned with the pain as soon as I did. "No. No ambulance."

"You stubborn..." I missed the rest of his words due to the pain in my head.

I raised a hand up and pressed it against my temple.

"You've been struck in the head. I think it might be a concussion."

"Hardy?"

"Shh. Yes, it's me. If you were more coherent, I'd be yelling at you right now."

"I called you," I said.

"You did. And thank goodness for that."

"You came." I smiled dumbly up at him, my vision blurring so there was two of him front of me.

He snorted. "I did."

"Did you see anything?"

"Just you lying in the middle of the street, you foolish, foolish thing."

An ambulance tore around the corner. "No hospital."

"Yes. You're going. For me. Because you are the bane of my existence."

I laughed, and it hurt so bad.

"Don't laugh," Hardy urged.

The paramedics jumped out and surrounded me. Hardy gently set my head down. "I'll come by the hospital."

He looked at the paramedics. "She is not fine, and she is not to drive herself home. Are we clear?"

The two of them gave each other a look and nodded. "Crystal," said one of them.

"Good." He got to his feet and jogged off into the dark.

Someone flashed a light in my eye. I groaned in pain.

"Definitely concussed," one of them said. "Ma'am, lay still. We're going to get a stretcher."

I THOUGHT about the wine still sitting on my coffee table as I grumbled internally about what a bummer it was to spend the night in the hospital and letting it go to waste.

The lights above me were too bright. Everything here was too bright. My head didn't hurt as bad as it had before probably because they'd given me something for the pain. I had to lay on the right side of my head because the left back side sported an enormous goose egg. I ran my fingers through my hair earlier and hissed in pain when I touched it.

The nurse clucked her tongue when she walked in and saw me. "Best leave that alone for at least the next few days. Whoever got you whacked you pretty hard."

"With what? A tree trunk?" I moaned.

She laughed prettily. "Doctor can't tell. Looks like something metal maybe. Like a can or something."

"Who carries a can in the street in the middle of winter?"

She came around to check my i.v. "That'd be the person who whacked you, honey."

I smiled weakly. "When can I get out of here?"

"Not until tomorrow morning at the earliest." She fluffed up my pillow and patted me on the arm. "That handsome detective stopped by a little while ago." She wiggled her eyebrows. "He seems way more concerned than he should be about someone he isn't sweet on."

"He's definitely not sweet on me. I think he's just concerned if I die, I'll come back and haunt him."

"She would," Hardy said as he stepped into the room. He held a small teddy bear.

"Mmm hmm," said the nurse and made her way out of the room.

"Does the teddy bear mean you aren't going to yell at me?" I asked hopefully.

"The concussion means I'm not going to yell at you. The teddy bear is because I know your head must be killing you."

He set it on the bedside table and took a seat. "Are you up for a chat?"

"I'm stuck in a hospital bed at your mercy."

He smiled, though it didn't quite reach his eyes. "First, I want to let you know I appreciate you calling me and telling me what happened."

"But?"

The morning sun was streaming into the windows of my room making burnished highlights stand out in Hardy's hair. His eyes looked bluer than usual, but his face was still tired.

"No but. I don't think you should have gotten out of your car, but I think you know it as well."

"I wanted to make sure she was okay."

"I know. Not a lot of people would have done the same, though."

"This is Silverwood Hollow. Most of us would have done it."

"I'll give you the benefit of the doubt."

"Did you find anything? The woman? The can?"

His brows drew together. I pointed to my head. "They think I got clocked with a can."

Hardy snorted. "No cans, I'm afraid." He looked away for a minute. "I found the woman, though."

My heart sank. "Something happened to her, didn't it?"

Silence loomed in the room, the only sound that of the beeping equipment.

"I'm afraid so." He met my eyes. "I found her body deeper into the woods."

I closed my eyes. Tears fell down my face. "I didn't see anyone else," I croaked out. "It was only her. No one was chasing her."

"I think maybe she'd already been hit and the adrenaline took her farther than she should have been able to go."

"Do you know who it was?"

He nodded. "Maria Fontenot."

I gasped. "The agent?"

"Yes. She was due to leave this morning. I can't piece together what happened yet, but I have people working on it."

"She knew something about Mary Ruth. I know it!"

He put a hand on my arm. "Settle down. You have a pretty bad concussion and you'll be in here for at least another day. This is your time to retire from this case. You've done enough."

"Someone else died. Of course I didn't do enough."

"Are you the one who killed her, then?" he asked.

My eyes widened. "Of course not!"

"Then even doing nothing would have been enough. It's time for my team to step in and finish this up. Your information was valuable to me and the team. From what we know now and finding Maria, our suspect list just got a lot more narrow. You need to take this time to rest. We're close to finding Mary Ruth's murderer."

He stood. "I'm glad you're okay."

I gave him a wobbly smile. "Thanks for helping me."

"Any time, Dakota."

Hardy left the room, leaving me with the thoughts about Maria and how terrible her last moments must have been. The person who hit me on the head had to be the same person who murdered both Mary Ruth and Maria. So why hadn't they taken me out?

Looking down at the tube still in my arm, maybe they thought they had.

That thought sobered me up for the rest of the day.

Betty came to see me in the hospital. I'd just finished watching another episode of Law and Order when the small woman came in. I blinked in surprise. She held a small bouquet and a bottle of water.

She plunked it down in front of me and held the flowers out. "Water that's not tap and something from the flower shop."

"Uh. Thank you." I put them on the pull away table.

Betty pulled a chair out and sat down. "I'm so glad you're okay."

"Me too."

From my face, she knew I was wondering why she was here.

"I'm here because I feel terrible about what happened to you! I know you're trying to help Martha, but is this all worth it?" Tears shone in her eyes. "Mary Ruth died a terrible death. I heard this morning they found a woman's body, too. All this death and despair. Don't you get tired of it?"

I stared at her. "Well, normally this place is one of the safest in the country. This is an anomaly."

Betty laughed then. "I've read about you in the paper the other day. That article was about you, wasn't it?"

Freaking Cole. I still wanted to murder him over that. I didn't acknowledge her words, but she talked enough for the both of us and plowed on speaking. "You've solved two murders now. That's amazing!"

"I didn't really solve either one," I protested. "It was more a matter of being in the right place at the right time."

"Nonsense. That reporter laid out what you did each time. You're a smart woman."

"Thank you." This visit was beginning to unnerve me.

"I'm just asking you to be careful. The car is packed outside and I'm heading back home in a couple of hours. Mary Ruth's killer is still out there, and I no longer feel safe here. Not after this morning's discovery."

I nodded. "I don't intentionally put myself in danger, you know."

"None of us ever do." She stood up. "Enjoy the flowers. I'll see you around, Dakota, okay?"

"Okay." And as soon as she'd arrived, she'd gone. Outside of my window, I saw Betty get into her car and pull away.

The oddness of her visit wouldn't leave me for quite a while, though.

SIXTEEN

Two days later, I stood inside Tattered Pages watching snow fall gently to the ground. A white Christmas. I put a hand over my heart and sighed. Everything looked magical in Silverwood Hollow.

Spirits were high, people were spending in all the shops. Harper's offer on the house was accepted, and I was out of the hospital. The lump on the back of my head still hurt like the dickens, but everything was slowly starting to get back to normal. I took pain meds first thing in the morning when I woke up because I was still getting headaches, but the doctor told me they should wear off soon.

I hadn't seen Hardy or Cole. No sign of Betty or Martha either.

I felt content, but there was still a high level of concern in my stomach because the murderer was still out there.

Harper brought in a fancy bottle of white grape juice

with a cork and everything. She'd poured us a glass, and we stood by the door watching the people bustle by.

"Any plans for Christmas?" she asked.

"Not really. I'll go over Mom's. She makes the ham and I usually take care of the sides. Corky brings the wine."

Harper snorted. "Speaking of her, how is that old crazy lady?"

I grinned. "She'd love to hear you say that. I haven't chatted with her in a while, but I would have heard if something happened. As far as I know, Corky is well stocked in libations and she should be bringing us even more over Christmas."

I straightened. "Speak of the devil," I said and moved away from the door.

Mom burst in with Corky and Gran. Harper's expression grew delighted.

"I wonder if she brought wine," Harper murmured to me just as Mom drew her in for a hug.

"Harper, honey! It's so good to see you. The last time I saw you was the last time I saw my daughter so..."

I winced. "Hi Mom."

She drew me into a lilac scented hug. "You've been away far too long."

"I'm sorry," I whispered.

Mom kissed me on the cheek. Gran came next and hugged me tightly. Then Corky drew me in. "Darling, this shop is so cute! You should have a whiskey bar." She looked around. "Or a coffee bar that has whiskey. Or margaritas. How about whiskey during the winter and margaritas in the summer?"

"I think that's a grand idea, Miss Corky," Harper said, grinning from ear to ear.

"Don't encourage delinquency, girls," my mother warned. She pulled off her scarf and gloves. "Now, show me to the spicy romance aisle. I have a lot of books I need to pick up. Book club is meeting again soon and I want to have options! Plus I just finished that one with that spicy duke." My mom shivered.

"Eww. Mom. Gross."

She swatted me with her gloves. "Like you're a saint. Don't forget. I knew what books you tried to hide from me when your hormones were all high."

My cheeks colored.

"Don't forget about the time I found that Johanna Lindsey book tucked under your pillow," Gran interjected. "That was some impressive man chest right there."

"Now that Fabio," Corky said with a dreamy smile, "that's a fine hunk of man meat there."

Mom laughed and took me by the arm. "Show me the best new books you have in stock, honey. I have gifts to buy."

I left Mom, Corky, and Gran to browse through the shop while I went back to the register and opened up my journal. I'd been sketching out some ideas for the shop. None of them were things I planned on pulling the trigger on right away, but maybe one day. When I had a little more money and when my life slowed down some.

The bell rang, and I looked up only to see Betty walking in. She didn't look happy today. Her steps were a little jerky, and she looked like she had a fever.

I came out from behind the register. "Betty. Are you okay?" I put an arm out to help her. She swayed on her feet. I looked outside to see if anyone was with her and saw a shorter man with a larger nose. We locked eyes and he put his head down and rushed away.

Weird.

"I'm fine." She looked around the shop. "Is anyone here?"

Harper stepped out from the back. Her brows drew together. "Dakota?"

"There are a few people here. Why?"

Betty took a step back. She reached behind her. I stilled and put my hands out when I saw what she was holding.

Her hands shook as she pointed the gun at me. "The water. Why didn't you drink the water?" Her lips trembled. Tears shone in her eyes.

"Water? What water?"

She shook the gun. "The water I brought you at the hospital."

"The -" Everything clicked into horrible clarity. "The water. You poisoned the water."

Fear rooted my feet to the floor. I no longer heard my mother, my grandmother, Harper, or my aunt. Blood rushed through my ears and everything sounded like a wind tunnel. "You killed Mary Ruth. And Maria."

"You should have drank the water." Betty looked around wildly. Harper stood frozen in place. "Why did you have to get involved?" She waved the gun around. "You should have left well enough alone and stayed out of it!"

My eyes swung wildly as I tried to locate my family. I couldn't see them anymore. I prayed they'd stay hidden as I tried to resolve this. "Martha asked me to get involved, Betty. But I wasn't close to figuring out it was you."

"You almost saw me!" she screeched.

"You hit me."

"I did. I thought it would be enough. But you woke up. And then you wouldn't drink the water!"

"I'm sorry. I'm sorry I didn't drink the water. You can still leave now, Betty. I thought you were gone anyway."

"I waited until you died. But you didn't."

Betty sounded completely off her rocker.

"I didn't. I'm so sorry."

"Arsenic works," she muttered. "He said it always works and it doesn't taste like anything. That's why she ate the muffin. He said she would. Mary Ruth said it was the best she'd ever had. Plus she ate the other stuff I gave her too."

My stomach rolled. Gran peered around the corner at us. She held her index finger to her lips. Like I would give her away. I prayed she'd stay put, but I knew that wasn't in Gran's nature.

Poppy came out from where Gran was and pranced up behind Betty. I dared not look at her.

"Why don't you put the gun down?" I said. "We can resolve this."

"We can't," she insisted. "We can't do anything because you didn't drink the water."

"I don't drink a lot of water, I'm afraid. I live in a state of perpetual dehydration."

Gran, Mom, and Corky slid out from behind the shelf. I had to keep talking, babbling, whatever to keep her from turning around and seeing them.

"I don't know why I do it. But I do. I drink way too much coffee and tea and never enough water. My doctor thinks I'm ruining my kidneys."

Betty blinked at me. "Shut up."

"Why did you do it?"

"Do what?"

The obvious. Kill two people. But Betty wasn't all there. Maybe she never had been. "Hurt Mary Ruth?"

"It was her fault! I never gave her Martha's story. She stole it from me and then said she'd blame me if she was ever caught! I couldn't leave her then. I didn't want to get into trouble. I'd get into so much trouble if someone thought I stole Martha's work. And it was good. So good. Way better than what Mary Ruth ever came up with. My husband found out. He started blackmailing Mary Ruth for money. She didn't know I was married to him. I didn't like it but I felt like she owed it to me for what she was doing to me. All over a book." Her lower lip trembled. "I don't even like dogs that much."

"I'm sorry she did that to you." I risked a peek outside

again but that man, her husband, was gone. I glanced behind Betty and saw Gran gesture. She had something silver in her hand. Poppy crept beside her. I said another prayer we'd all get out of this alive.

Just as Gran raised whatever she had in her hand up, Betty stilled and spun. She saw Gran and raised the gun.

Poppy screeched louder than I'd ever heard her and struck at Betty's legs. The woman howled in pain as Poppy scratched and bit her.

The gun went off.

I lunged toward Betty, a scream tearing from my throat. I couldn't bear to see if the bullet had hit anyone yet. I had to focus on disarming her.

All I could hear was screaming and Poppy hissing as Betty tried to get away from her and me too. My fingers locked around the cold metal of the gun. Pain bloomed in the back of my head as I exerted myself way more than I should have.

But this was no longer a matter of me meddling. This was a matter of life and death and saving my family.

I put all the weight I could against Betty. Hands, so many hands, locked onto the weapon. I smelled my mother's perfume beside me. Tears streamed down my face as we went toppling.

Another bullet fired. A sob tore out of me.

The door blew open behind us. Frigid air blew in against the back of my neck and still all I heard was screaming.

I didn't know it at the time, but most of the noise came from me.

Betty sobbed underneath me. She bucked like a bull as she tried to get away. Finally, finally, the gun started to slip from her fingers but before I could take it, someone put their hand on mine.

"Let me."

And then the gun slipped away, and Betty rolled away, and I lay in a heap on the ground crying.

"Mom? Mom!"

"Shhh. It's okay. Everyone is okay." I opened my eyes only to see my mother crouched down beside me, worry in her blue eyes as she stroked my hair away from my face.

Cole stood above her, pointing the gun down at Betty.

"Harper!" he barked. "Call 911."

EPILOGUE

My palm needed stitches from the gun. Mom, Corky, Harper, and I all sat in the back of the ambulance. Trudy and Jen stood a few feet away, worry lines etched into their faces.

Worried townspeople milled around, all stunned at what had just happened in my store.

I saw Hardy's cruiser pull up. He stepped out of it, and his gaze bore into my soul.

"He's going to yell at me," I whispered as the paramedic put the last stitch in.

"If he does, you tell him to call me." I looked to my left only to see Everett Adams standing there.

I blinked in surprise. "Hi."

"Hi." He wore a new pair of jeans this time. Not splashed with chai. And a warm blue sweater with a white and blue scarf. I'd never seen a more color coordinated man.

"What are you doing here?"

Everett shrugged. "I was in the neighborhood. Kind of." His nose wrinkled adorably. "Okay, I'm lying. I came by to see you only to hear gunshots." He laughed, but it sounded forced. "I thought what are the odds Dakota is involved in that." He jerked a thumb at Cole. "When I saw this guy run straight for the only bookshop in town, I knew."

"Well, welcome to Silverwood Hollow," I said weakly.

Mom patted me on the hand and whispered something to Gran and my aunt. They slipped away just as Hardy walked up. His eyes took me in then slid to Everett.

"Dakota."

"Hey Hardy."

"You okay?"

I held up my palm. "Ten stitches."

He grunted. "I'll want to talk to you when this is over. Understand?"

"I do."

"We found her husband, too. There's nothing more to worry about."

I nodded my thanks. He gave me one long look, then turned to Everett.

"Keep her out of trouble?"

Everett's eyes widened. "I don't know about that. I've known her less than a day and she's managed to get a concussion, stitches, and shot at."

Hardy gave him a fierce grin. "That's right. Remember

that when you try to tell her what to do." He glanced once more back at me. "She's a fighter."

I blinked at his back and watched him walk away, my pulse fluttering in my neck. What in the world was that about?

And how could I get some more of it?

ALSO BY S.E. BABIN

A Shelf Indulgence Cozy Mystery Series

How about a ghost whisperer in a new magical town? Check out
The Psychic Cleaner series!

Psychic Cleaner

Like a little more magic with your cozies? Check out The
Magical Soapmaker Mysteries!

The Magical Soapmaker Mysteries

If you'd like a little more action and sass and don't mind some
PG-13 language, check out my Aphrodite series.

The Goddess Chronicles

Or, if you like a snarky bartender with a secretive mixed heritage,
meet Violet!

Cocktails in Hell

ABOUT THE AUTHOR

Sheryl is a tired middle aged college student. Send coffee. Or wine. Whatever. Just make sure it's a stimulant.